AULD LANG STEIN

A KATIE MURPHY COZY MYSTERY

SUZANNE BOLDEN

CHAPTER ONE

The clock was ticking, and in a matter of minutes, it would be midnight. It had been almost a year since Paddy's Pub opened its doors, and the happy faces gathered here tonight were proof of its success. For me, Katie Murphy, tonight was as much a celebration of the new year ahead as of Maeve and Paddy's success in bringing the warm, welcoming atmosphere of the Irish pubs from their childhood to this small town on the shore of the Gulf of Mexico.

Paddy was in his element, raising his beer stein and toasting with everyone in celebration of the year ahead. Maeve's face radiated joy as she bustled around the room, ensuring that the food and drinks were plentiful and delicious for all their guests.

A chill rain had been falling when I arrived, but

within the last hour, it had stopped and now, happily, Seaside Cove's fireworks display could proceed. Inside the pub, there was a cozy warmth and a joyful atmosphere. The staff had moved our mannequin, affectionately named Mel, from his post outside the front door and brought him inside the lobby so his tuxedo and top hat wouldn't get ruined.

Platters of delectable savory dishes were constantly replenished throughout the evening as guests mingled around the buffet table. Some of our regular patrons were almost unrecognizable as they'd adorned themselves with fancy evening wear and jewelry. The dance floor was illuminated with crystal beams from the slowly twirling disco ball, and the band I'd booked months ago was perfect for the mixed-age crowd we had. They covered everything from Glen Miller to Michael Jackson.

My home was here now, and I couldn't be happier. Raven, my sweet furry companion, knew her way around the pub and was curled up in one of our cozy booths. I didn't recognize the elderly couple she'd intruded on, but they didn't seem to mind her presence. The woman absentmindedly stroked her back as Raven stretched out for a scratch.

A circle of clapping dancers had formed around someone in the middle of the dance floor. It was Winnie

Stanley, who'd tamed her crazy curls by pinning them up and adding a huge sparkly gold bow. She lifted the hem of her black dress, freeing her feet to dance the Irish jig to the lively music playing. In her other hand, she carried her glittery gold flats. Her bare feet moved with surprising agility for a woman of her size. The onlookers around the circle cheered and whooped as she paused to catch her breath. Despite their pleas for an encore, she waved them off and took a seat in her chair, panting slightly from the energetic dance.

"Winnie, I'm speechless," I said.

"Honey, this is the best shindig I've been to in a coon's age, but I need to sit a spell before my feet fall clean off!"

"Looks like you could use a drink."

"Well, Katie, the way I ended up with my shoes in my hand was 'cause of drink," she drawled out. "But a nice cold glass of water would do me mighty good right now."

Liam, our head bartender, was swamped with work tonight, so Aubrey had decided to pitch in by busing tables and loading the glassware in the dishwasher behind the bar to help him out. Their relationship was developing beyond just friendship. This made me happy because Liam was a cousin direct from Ireland and Aubrey was my friend and my landlord to boot.

"Here's a water for our dancing queen," Aubrey said. "Party's really hopping!"

Most of my book club members were here, too. Marge Shaw brought her husband Ken along, but they had left earlier. Marge said she wanted to watch the fireworks in their bedroom. She laughed at my shocked expression, saying she meant the town's midnight fireworks from their bedroom window...not where my mind had taken me!

Vivian Trimble, our former mayor's wife, didn't show up, though. She admitted she still felt uncomfortable here in the pub where her dear Vinnie had died, and she just couldn't bear it. Hannah Brooks-Nelson, the owner of our local newspaper, came with her husband Greg, and I lost track of how many times I saw them out on the dance floor.

A regal but empty gilded frame hung from the ceiling, its golden edges catching the light cast against it. The numbers of the new year, bold and black, were suspended below, seemingly floating in the air. It beckoned guests to step behind it and capture the memory with a photograph. A moment frozen in time, filled with joy and anticipation for what's to come.

As I walked by, Loretta Quinn, Peaches Kershaw, Eve Brooks, and an old high school friend who was in town for a memorial service crowded together, laughing and acting silly as one of our hostesses snapped photos reminiscent of the old photo booths they must have used as kids.

Jesse Shaw was in town with a group of anglers chasing after bass, as this was the prime month for catching them in the Wimico River. Ever since the Halloween incident, when he was with me during the Dexter Fortinelli scuffle, he had been busy. I only saw him sporadically, and tonight he had his hands full with entertaining his guests.

The stroke of midnight must be approaching because Maeve hurried around, distributing noisemakers, feathered headbands, and plastic top hats to everyone in preparation for the countdown. The band began to play the familiar tune of Auld Lang Syne. Above the dance floor, a net of gold and silver balloons waited to be released when the clock hit midnight.

I stood next to Maeve as Paddy began to shout.

Ten, nine, eight, seven...

The crowd picked up the count.

Six, five, four...

The room lights dimmed.

Three, two...

For a deliciously sweet second, we stayed in the past year...

One!

And the new year arrived in Seaside Cove!

The din of noisemakers, whistles, shouts, and cheers sounded. Then, clear as a bell, the singer slowly began the song.

Should old acquaintances be forgot and never brought to mind,

The crowd joined in.

We'll take a cup of kindness yet,

For auld lang syne.

Eve, Loretta, Peaches, and their friend reached for each other's hands, swaying to the lovely words of the Scottish folk song.

And there's a hand, my trusty friend!

And give me a hand o' thine!

Those holding a glass, whether a champagne flute, a cocktail glass, or a beer stein, held their drinks high.

And we'll take a good-will draught,

For auld lang syne.

Paddy took Maeve in his arms and bent her back, kissing her as the singer repeated the chorus.

For auld lang syne my dear,

We'll take a cup of kindness yet,

Across the room, I smiled, seeing Liam and Aubrey sharing a kiss.

The singer's beautiful rendition came to an end with her holding onto the notes of the final words...

For auld lang syne.

I looked up to watch the balloon drop. I was overcome with a sense of belonging.

Suddenly, I felt hands on my shoulders, turning me around.

CHAPTER TWO

It was Jesse. "Happy New Year, gorgeous." Jesse gave me a kiss that lingered an extra second before he pulled back and met my gaze. "I hope I didn't overstep."

Before I could respond, a burst of balloons filled the air, and a loud cheer erupted from the crowd around us, startling me. But his strong hands gently held my shoulders steady as a hot flush crossed my cheeks. "I've got to get back to my group of guests, but I've been looking forward to giving you that kiss all day."

I shook myself to clear my head and reached up to hug Jesse, wishing him a Happy New Year. He turned to walk away but glanced back over his shoulder with a wink toward me. I couldn't stop the smile that spread across my face. It was definitely a good start to the new year.

The air filled with the sound of cheerful greetings and wishes for a prosperous year ahead. Warm hugs and kisses were exchanged amongst friends and family all across the pub. The night was alive with anticipation for what the future held.

Jack and Sophia Daniels came over, and they each gave me a friendly peck on my cheek. "This is the best party," Sophia said. "You Irish sure do know how to bring in the New Year. Want to join us outside to watch the fireworks?"

"Sure," I said, following as they worked their way through the crowd inside Paddy's Pub to emerge onto Main Street, where others gathered to witness the colorful explosions lighting up the night sky above the bay. On the soft grassy lawns of the park, I imagined little ones snuggled up on blankets, their eyes fighting against drowsiness but now opening wide at the first pops and crackles of color in the sky.

We found Sophia's brother Scott with his arms wrapped tightly around his wife Jackie, who snuggled back against his chest. "This sure beats the ice and cold during the winter in Wisconsin," he said. "Glad we made it down here for the holidays this year."

Watching them, a couple well into their sixties, who'd only been married a year and were still exhibiting a newlywed vibe, touched my heart. An unexpected pang of longing shot through me. What was in store for me in the romance department? I was right to leave Joel the Jerk back in Los Angeles. He wasn't capable of loving anyone but himself. Still, sometimes…

But for now, I turned back to the fireworks, trying to push away any negative thoughts. The vibrant colors and loud bursts were distracting enough to quickly lift my spirits again. Here, in the midst of the community crowd, all eyes turned skyward toward the dazzling fireworks slicing through the night sky. The sound of oohs and ahs echoed through the air, mingling with the crackling of sparks and the booming of explosions. Burst after colorful burst filled the dark canvas above the glistening water. The display grew, building up to a grand finale that left us all breathless with shared awe.

When it was all over, and the crowd began to disburse, the five of us made our way back inside the pub for a nightcap. The band was playing for another hour, and the buffet had been freshened up with delectable deserts and coffee.

Paddy joined us for a moment. "Ready for our big night on the water, Jackie? It'll be my first time out this year."

"Ah, seriously? No, wait, I get you now, very funny!" Jackie said.

"Hey, are you running around on me already?" Scott teased.

"Oh, my dear, fear not, you are invited along. Paddy offered to escort me on his fishing boat up the river so I could take photographs of the full moon's light on the river. It will be a perfect addition to my newest project about life on the Wimico."

"For a display at Parker Photography?" I admired Jackie's photographic works.

"Yes, for a display back in my studio at Harmony, but I hope to exhibit it here as well," Jackie explained. "And I'm thinking about publishing a coffee-table book featuring the area's natural beauty, along with its charming cottages, weathered faces, and fishing boats. There are endless opportunities to capture the spirit of this area."

Scott smiled down at his wife. "We love it here, and with my sister and Jack now proud owners of a second home, we hope to visit often in this little corner of the world."

"Oh, and Katie, we'll be here a few days yet, so I hope you can take me out to see where Ella Winchester has her art studio," Jackie said.

"I'd be happy to. It's not the typical studio of an artist, but I just know you'll love her place in the forest. Would Wednesday work for you?"

"Remember, we have that outing planned to St. John Island that afternoon," Jack said.

"So let's shoot for Wednesday morning and I'll have you back before lunch. See you then," I said before leaving to help with some of the cleanup as the pub emptied out.

It had been a long night. The fireworks were over. And it was a new year. I had thought of making a resolution but not narrowed it down to a practical and achievable one.

Aubrey had resolved to explore more of the clutter of antiques and unique objects left behind by her great-aunt, who she inherited her old mansion from. Renting the second floor from Aubrey was perfect. I loved being able to look down at the community park and out over the bay to Horseshoe Island. Aubrey and I often met up on my balcony for morning coffee or her backyard fire pit for evening wine.

Raven and I said goodnight to the cleanup staff and rode the short distance home in my go-to vehicle here, a golf cart.

Life was simpler here and much more satisfying than running my own party-planning business back in Los Angeles. Leaving the hectic and competitive environment of LA and a cheating boyfriend behind was the right choice. Running parties and events here at Paddy's

Pub satisfied my creative side. And until recently, I'd not missed having a boyfriend in my life.

A text message popped up on my phone, sending a small wave of happiness through me as I read…

I got a lot of new year's kisses and hugs from the beach crowd here at rum runners wish one of them would have been from you. happy new year tyler

…and saw the heart emoji at the end of it.

I quickly texted back. *would have been nice.* My finger paused as I considered what emoji to add. Don't overthink this, Katie. Just click the dang heart. Everyone uses hearts all over the place. But instead, I chose the blowing-a-kiss emoji and added *the best I can do* and a laughing emoji after it.

CHAPTER THREE

Located just inside the front entrance of Paddy's Pub, the Coffee Corner had its own regulars. It provided a nice balance to the pub that opened for lunch and dinner, operating well into the night. Maeve was the queen of this space, selling her own freshly baked goods and those from Betty's Bakery on the west side. It had been a late night for me, but I promised Maeve I'd handle this morning's opening so she and Paddy could sleep in or at least enjoy some morning peace and quiet together at Kenmare Cottage, their cute little home.

Well wishes for a happy and healthy new year could be heard as I poured coffee, pulled donuts and cupcakes out of the display case, and prepared tea for the customers coming through the door.

"Mel's looking a little under the weather," Eve teased. "He didn't get much sleep either, did he?"

"He asked me if I could spare an aspirin this morning," I said with a grin. "Poor guy. All the people hanging on him just to get a photograph."

Eve was here with Peaches and Loretta and waited for their friend from out of state, who was on her way over from the Fulton Inn. I knew that they were gathered to honor a dear friend who'd recently passed away and designated the group to spread her ashes at sites around Seaside Cove.

"I thought she might have stayed with one of you," I said, pouring coffees all around.

"I didn't offer," Loretta said. "She would have jabbered my ear off. And all about herself. It gets tiring."

Peaches poured two sugar packets into her coffee. "My husband doesn't care for overnight guests. And doesn't like staying overnight at anyone's place either. Remember those sleepovers the sisters used to have? My god what our parents put up with."

"You were the silliest, Peaches. That lip-syncing you did had us all cracking up. I offered her a room in my place, but she refused. Whatever, she might be just more comfortable in a hotel." Eve waved to someone walking by on the street. "Here's Betty Jo now."

The woman who came through the door was well

put together, wearing a navy cardigan over a simple white shirt and jeans. Betty Jo's chestnut hair was expertly styled, likely a result of an expensive cut. However, she was due for another color as there were signs of gray starting to peek through at the roots. Despite her flawlessly applied makeup, there was a hint of weariness evident in the shadows under her eyes and a dullness to her complexion. She had a slight thickness around her midsection, a common occurrence for women in her age group. But none of these imperfections could hide the fact that she possessed a timeless beauty.

"Good morning, sisters one and all. Quite a party you threw last night for my arrival," she said before pulling out the chair left for her and hanging her designer bag on the back of it.

"Why thank you," Peaches said with a big grin. "We felt it came together rather well."

"Okay, so just what is this sister thing you all have going on?" I asked after taking Betty Jo's order of black coffee.

"We were best friends throughout high school. All six of us decided to call ourselves the Secret Sisters," Peaches said. "What a wonderful time we had growing up here in Seaside Cove. Whispering in the halls about boyfriends. Dances in the gym."

With a shoulder shaking shiver, Betty Jo said, "Oh please, that sweaty, smelly gym. Yech! How could I forget it? And those first awkward fast dances. My God, the guys were horrible dancers." She took her seat and paused as a slow, suggestive smile appeared on her lips. "Though I do recall several very sexy slow dances."

"Yuck," Loretta said. "The guys all nervous with sweaty palms. And just wanting to get so close and grabby."

Betty Jo reached for the plate of pastries the group had ordered. "I don't remember that part of it."

"You wouldn't," Eve said. "If my memory serves me, you always seemed to be dancing with the cutest hunky ones."

"Didn't all us cheerleaders do that, though? We had a certain image to maintain." Betty Jo accepted the cup of coffee from me. "It was expected of us."

"Not me," Peaches said, clasping her hands to her heart and rocking back and forth. "Bobby was my one and only all through high school and beyond."

"Yeah, right," Loretta said. "You two broke up junior year. I remember you gave him his class ring back."

"I did not!"

Betty Jo burst out laughing. "She's right because I remember that was the time because he asked me out."

Peaches's face contorted into a deep frown, her brow

furrowed in denial of the truth. "He did not," she insisted vehemently.

Betty Jo's quiet snort of laughter did not go unnoticed by Peaches, but she chose to ignore it, taking a huge bite of her almond croissant.

"Ladies, how about we save the reminiscing until we meet here for dinner tonight?" Eve said. "Chris Pratt asked that we meet him under the stands at the high school football field in half an hour. That's the first spot his mother Linda requested her ashes be spread."

"The whole thing with spreading ashes is getting out of hand," Betty Jo said. "What's the big deal about it? I'm more of an advocate of the traditional way of handling those sorts of things."

Linda had passed away recently, and now I only counted four women. "Peaches, didn't you just say there were six of you? Are you expecting one more person to arrive for this memorial?"

A veil of sadness momentarily dropped over the four women gathered here before Eve looked up at me and started to explain that one of the Secret Sisters had passed away only two years after high school.

Betty Jo interrupted. "It was such a sad thing for all of us. Tilly's body was found on Bonfire Beach. That was our hangout spot on the river. It had a small fishing pier with a sandy beach. We spent hours jumping off the pier into the river or using the rope that hung from a sturdy tree on the shore to throw ourselves far out into the deep water. Big old stone fire pit, too. Yummy roasted marshmallows!"

"I'm sorry to hear that," I said. "What happened to her?"

"She drowned," Loretta said. "Poor thing was…"

"But it wasn't an accident." Betty Jo butted in again. "To this day, it's considered a cold case. Come to think of it, Linda Pratt was Tilly's roommate here in Seaside Cove. You see, Katie, some of us went on to higher education, but Tilly didn't. I and Eve ended up being dorm mates at the University of Florida at Gainesville."

"But back to Tilly," Loretta said, rolling her eyes. "The police had a hard time finding any suspects other than her boyfriend. Eventually, they tried to pin it on him. Lover's quarrel or something like that, they said. He's the one who found her. He was supposed to meet up with her that night, but when he got there, he found her body. Jimmy claimed he saw someone running away, but that went nowhere as far as the law was concerned."

"Why is it a cold case if he did it?" I asked.

"He didn't do it," Peaches said. "The jury didn't convict him. But he was never the same after losing Tilly and with the shame of everyone thinking he was her murderer."

Betty Jo pursed her red-painted lips. "And the autopsy revealed she was pregnant."

"That's in the past. Right now, we'd better get going," Eve said. "Chris wants to go to the beach on Horseshoe Island after the football field."

"Oh, for goodness' sake. What's next?" Betty Jo asked. "He's making this such a big deal."

"There is a third spot, but Chris is saving it for tomorrow when he's giving us each a personal packet from Linda," Peaches said as she finished her final sip of coffee. "It'll probably be sad, especially knowing she put them together during her illness."

Eve nodded. "I agree. She could be a little over the top about keeping track of things in everyone's life story, but the world needs people like her who remember and memorialize events."

"Linda the historian," Betty Jo snipped. "I should have figured she'd do something like this."

No one could have missed the sound of Loretta slamming her hands on the table before shoving back to stand. With a tight set to her lips, she excused herself to use the restroom, telling the others she'd meet them outside.

In a few minutes, Loretta passed back by the arched opening to the coffee shop.

"Sorry about your friend, but I'll see you all later," I said.

Loretta paused to take a deep breath. "Maybe, if I don't end up losing my cool because of Mrs. Betty Jo Turner and her…" And through gritted teeth, she added, "It is so tempting to strangle her just to shut her up."

CHAPTER FOUR

When other staff arrived, I headed up to our second-floor office to take care of a few things there. Maeve and Paddy sent a text with a photo of them enjoying a walk in their neighborhood. Maeve added a note pointing out that she had resolved to lose weight during the year ahead, and these were the first steps, ending with a laughing emoji.

I completed a budget proposal for an April wedding ceremony, and dinner planned for our rooftop venue. Construction of the rooftop deck seemed to be moving along smoothly and our general contractor, Roger Collins, had assured us that it would be completed in plenty of time.

Grace Norris's email about marketing plans for her new guest house was fun to see. Her enthusiasm was contagious. She hired a marketing firm to create branding for her, and the options she was given were very appealing. Her email also included how we might benefit each other with shared promotional opportunities and materials. Her final notes were on possible opening dates that Roger, also the general contractor on the updates at the conversion of the McCracken mansion to a bed-and-breakfast, had given her and Ruby. He was a busy man again. After the debacle on Halloween, he'd sincerely apologized and regrouped.

My friend and landlord, Aubrey, was also our accountant. I went over the projected year-end numbers she provided us. As part owner here, it was gratifying to see how well the business was doing. My nest egg from selling my LA party planning business was intact, and I'd been able to add to it as the past months went by.

With office tasks wrapped up, I decided to head home to tend to a few chores that were building up there. Maybe this would be my New Year's resolution. Stop procrastinating!

* * *

As I stripped my bed sheets, Raven, my mischievous cat, playfully tumbled around inside them, desperately trying to grab my attention. Her fluffy black tail peaked out, flicking back and forth as she darted between the layers of fabric, daring me to find her hidden form. I couldn't help but smile as she paused in between her antics, waiting for me to uncover her hiding spot amongst the crumpled linens.

The next hour was spent video chatting with Mom and Dad back in Ireland. With them being five hours ahead of me, I tried to avoid catching them at dinner time. Raven stuck her nose in as usual, prancing back and forth between me and the image of them on my computer. They got such a kick out of her.

Seeing the Secret Sisters come together today reminded me of my own high school friends. It had been ages since we last caught up. Mom said they always asked about me whenever she saw them in town. Maybe this was another idea for a resolution. Be better at keeping in touch with people I love.

"Mom, could you get their phone numbers for me, please? I'd love to catch up with them."

"Aye, dearie," she replied. I noticed her lean over to jot down the names I gave her.

"Think you'll forget that quickly?" I asked.

"The memory isn't what it used to be," she answered, looking around the tabletop and turning toward the kitchen counter behind them.

I saw Dad's face come close to the screen.

"She has a hard time rememberin' where her glasses are. Usually, she finds 'em..." And he tapped himself atop his head with a wink.

Mom laughed as she reached for her reading glasses, which were indeed right on top of her head, before pushing Dad aside from hogging the screen. "Never mind that old fool. He's just as bad."

"Say hi to me brother and Maeve," Dad called out as Mom blew a kiss, and our call ended.

Gosh, but I missed them! But at least I still got to see their goofy banter from halfway around the world.

Inside the restaurant, all evidence of the partying last night was gone. Things were quiet, and a few regulars sat at the rounded corner of the bar chatting with Paddy.

"Hey, I thought you were taking the day off."

"I did. Didn't ya get that snap of us takin' a stroll?" Paddy asked. "Me mates here called me in for a pint to ring in the new year. They're not ones for partying on New Year's Eve, so I couldn't refuse."

One of the men protested, saying Paddy had called them.

He rubbed his chin. "Aye, I might've. But Maeve

didn't want me hangin' around all day. Her and Winnie were working on their gardens. They're putting in a path between our houses, so Winnie doesn't have to push through the bushes to stop by."

"Talked to Dad today and they say hi."

"That's lovely. How's me brother doing?" Paddy asked.

"He's good. They're doing some remodeling, so that's keeping them busy." I wished Paddy's buddies a Happy New Year and went to talk with Eve and Peaches, sitting at a corner table near the window.

"How'd the day with your friends go?" I asked, taking in the fact that the table was set for only two.

"Interesting, to say the least," Eve said. "We'd all planned on coming here for dinner, but Loretta and Betty Jo opted out."

"And Chris was going back to Shaw's to get a little fishing in." Peaches patted the seat next to her for me. "Park yourself here for a minute."

The waitress came by and asked if I needed anything. I was starting to say no, but Peaches stepped in, asked for another wine glass, and began to tell me about their day. "It didn't go well. I felt bad for Chris. There was a very awkward encounter. You remember what we told you about our sister who died young? Well, at the high school football field, we ran into Tilly's sister, Frances

Eastwood. She's some sort of janitor or cleaning person and doing some extra work while school is closed for winter break."

"Bet she was glad to run into her sister's friends," I said.

"One might think that." Eve paused to reach for the bottle of wine on their table and pour me a glass. "But that is not how it went. Not even close. In an unpleasant way, she asked what we were doing there. Betty Jo took on the task of explaining the situation to Frances, or as she was called, to Frankie."

"Suppose that didn't help," I said.

"Correct. It only made things worse. You could see Frankie getting more upset the longer Betty Jo talked," Peaches said.

Eve nodded in agreement. "Then, out of the blue, she lashed out at our entire group for failing to protect their so-called sister. Telling us in no uncertain terms that she was a real sister to Tilly. Not some pretend aren't-we-all-great-buddies kind of sister. Frankie said she knew we weren't sharing all we knew about that day. And she stabbed a finger directly in Betty Jo's chest as she said it."

Peaches pursed her lips. "Oh, that got Betty Jo riled up. Even left a smudge on her nice white shirt."

"Next, Frankie brought up one of my books, *Where*

the Road Ends, claiming I'd used their family's tragedy to further my career."

"Ouch. That's rude," I said.

Eve swirled her wineglass, watching the deep red liquid move in circles. "She had a point about the book. I used our Secret Sisters club as inspiration, but I certainly did not incorporate any of the things she was accusing me of. She's such a bitter, angry woman."

Eve went on to explain that the bad vibes followed them to the beach on Horseshoe Island, where Loretta and Betty Jo got into a heated argument about Betty Jo leaving the University of Florida in her junior year to go to Emory in Atlanta. She was lording that over Loretta, who decided to get a job in Tallahassee and attend Tallahassee State College at night. Loretta got hot and shot back that she had been relieved to hear that Betty Jo moved further away because that meant she'd come back to Seaside Cove less frequently.

"Chris was just standing there wide-eyed, taking it all in," Peaches said. "We had this beautiful beach in front of us. The Gulf waters sparkling. The seagulls calling. And there goes Betty Jo, spoiling the entire day. That's when Chris announced he was going back to Shaw's for some fishing he had lined up. In my opinion, he just wanted out of there. Away from his mother's crazy friends."

"And that's when he said the thing that really fired up Betty Jo," Eve said. "He told us he'd see us in the morning at Bonfire Beach to wrap up his trip here."

"That's the beach where Tilly died, right?" I asked. "Wow, that'll be different. The other two spots held happy memories for all of you."

"So had the beach at one time. We spent wonderful afternoons and evenings there together," Peaches said, her voice slipping away. "Until Tilly's body was found."

There was a river my friends and I used to gather at back in Ireland. I couldn't even imagine what it must have felt like for the group when they lost one of their own at such a young age. "So, what happened next?"

Eve gazed across the warmly lit, cozy pub and recounted how Betty Jo had exploded at Chris, accusing Linda of forcing them to relive painful memories. He said he had no idea what memories she was complaining about. This was what his mother wanted, and he'd be darned if he didn't fulfill her wishes. Loretta then chided her that she should stop making it all about herself. To which Betty Jo dramatically suggested that Loretta keep her bleeping opinions to herself and should try walking a mile in her shoes. And with one last jab, Loretta added that she would never put her foot in Betty Jo's stinky shoe.

Eve and I both were shocked when we heard Peaches

choking down giggles. "Watching Betty Jo react, all I could think about was Wile E. Coyote and how his eyes would narrow into a piercing glare with his brow creating deep creases across his forehead. He'd get so mad at the Road Runner that his ears would twitch, and he'd flush up red with anger."

Eve laughed out loud. "Perfect image of what she looked like. Especially when Loretta turned to us and said that Ms. Betty Jo Kunkle Turner needed to do some hard thinking about her memories before she stomped away."

"So, it's just us two tonight," Peaches summarized. "I'm going to call Loretta later and see how she's doing."

"I wonder if Betty Jo will even show up tomorrow," Eve murmured. "Soon, she and Chris will go back to where they came from, and we can get back to our happy little life here in Seaside Cove."

But unforeseen events during the night ahead would take away the possibility of that happening anytime soon.

CHAPTER FIVE

Jackie came along with me and Raven on our golf cart drive to drop off Ella Winchester's income from sales of her December artwork and Tupelo honey in the Coffee Corner. Despite my attempts to convince her otherwise, Ella still preferred to keep her money in cash instead of opening a checking account. Which was fine with me because it gave me a wonderful excuse to see her. I loved the peaceful drive up River Road, with the sunlight filtering through the trees and the fresh morning air moving against us.

As we drove past the entrance to Shaw's River Lodge Jackie mentioned that she had seen it from the river last night during her photography excursion with Paddy. "It looked like a charming old lodge. Good for a future photography trip to capture the historic feeling of the old fishing camps here on the river."

"I'm not sure how long it has been around, but the Shaw family has operated it for at least three generations." Memories of Jesse's midnight kiss flitted across my mind, and I almost missed the narrow gravel road that would take us to Ella's.

When the gravel drive ended, I explained that we had to walk the rest of the way. Jackie paused under the intricately woven vine arch to take in the details of feathers, reeds, and dried flowers laced into it. "Wow, how clever. So simple yet so beautiful."

We entered under it and strolled quietly along the pathway, serenaded by chirping birds and buzzing insects. Coming to the opening to Ella's yard, Jackie hesitated. "Unbelievable. What a magical place."

I understood what she was experiencing, the calm tranquility and peaceful existence one felt here. Cows and horses outside of their small barn, grazing in the pasture. Chickens moving together, quietly pecking the ground for food. Goats alerted to our presence, meandering in our direction. And in nooks and corners, the surprise of her artistic touches added to the natural landscape.

The two women had met before but never here. Jackie

listened attentively as Ella walked the grounds with Raven trailing behind. The two of them were kindred souls, both appreciating creative expression. When they returned to where I sat, I was delighted to learn that Jackie had talked Ella into coming back to Seaside Cove with us and joining her on the boat ride out to St. John's Island.

"I'm so happy for you, Ella. You should find an abundance of driftwood and shells to collect there."

"Yes, since it's been uninhabited for so long, it's my kind of place," Ella said. "Let me get one of my collection baskets, and I'll be right back out."

As we drove away in my golf cart, the only sound was the gravel crunching under the wheels on Ella's road. It wasn't until we were almost back to River Road that I noticed the distant sound of sirens, and Ella called out, "Stop, Katie. Listen. Something terrible is happening to someone you know."

My mind immediately leaped to Jesse, and I looked toward Ella. She shook her head, and I let out a breath of relief. We had experienced this strange mental connection before. It was hard to define what I thought Ella possessed. Was it ESP...extra sensory perception?

Or a high level of intuition? Was she a clairvoyant or just super sensitive?

Whichever, I sped up until I could see the sign for Shaw's in the distance. A little further south, we caught sight of the flashing emergency lights reflecting off the trees. Their hard, abrasive siren sounds suddenly silenced.

As we approached, we noticed two other vehicles parked at a small turnoff. One car I recognized as belonging to Eve. The other vehicle had Georgia license plates.

We followed paramedics carrying medical gear past the *No Trespassing* signs and along a weed-covered, seldom-used path. A police officer raced ahead of them on foot, one hand holding down his holster and the other hanging on to his hat.

When we arrived at a clearing where the tall bushes and trees ended, we saw the Wimico River flowing silently by, edged by a sliver of inviting sandy beach. A rickety wooden fishing pier jutted out over the water, its rough planks worn down by time and weather. A small wooden fishing shack stood to the side, its walls peeling and green moss-covered roof sagging with age, a relic of simpler times.

Where the pier and the land met, a lifeless form lay

tangled in overgrown weeds, nestled against the decaying pilings.

CHAPTER SIX

One. Two. Three. Three of the Secret Sisters, along with a middle-aged man, gathered near the body.

The police officer began to gently assist a kneeling Peaches to stand upright, but her knees gave out.

"Can you ladies please help move your friend away from the body?" the officer asked. "We need to preserve the scene."

Eve and Loretta managed to get Peaches standing and move her to a grassy knoll where she could sit and lean back against a tree stump.

Eve approached me. "What are you doing here, Katie?"

"We saw the ambulance and police car. Who is that woman?"

"Betty Jo," Eve murmured, looking back toward the

tragic scene. "She must have arrived early this morning. Chris found her like this when he got here."

My knees felt weak now, too, and my breath slowed as I took in the gravity of the scene in front of me.

The pier.

The memories.

The charred ring of stones.

The frayed rope dangling from the strong tree limb.

Paramedics approached the body, feeling for a pulse, then quietly backing away to wait.

Chris, Linda's son, spoke to the officer. I caught snippets of him explaining who he was and why he was here. We heard him confirm that she was dead when he arrived this morning.

Darnell arrived next, surprised to see us all here in this remote spot. He walked over to observe the body and its position and briefly talked to the officer and Chris before walking in our direction.

"Mr. Pratt explained why he was here with you three." Darnell turned to where Ella, Jackie, and I stood and asked, "But why are you other three here?"

"We were on the River Road when we heard the emergency vehicles. I had a feeling that wherever they were headed, we should go there to help," Ella said in her soft, gentle voice.

Chief Darnell began questioning Loretta, Peaches,

and Eve. Did they know next of kin? Was the victim in town by herself? When was the last time we saw her? His questions were focused and delivered briskly.

Eve spoke first. "We were all together yesterday. But late in the afternoon, Betty Jo complained of a headache and went back to her room at the Fulton Inn. We didn't see or hear from her after that. She came to Seaside Cove alone, to our knowledge."

"A headache, you say. Was she unsteady? Ill? Anything that might have caused her to fall into the water?"

"Not that I'm aware of," Eve said, shaking her head slowly. "We haven't seen each other for years, so I couldn't really say how physically stable she is, but she certainly looked okay to us on New Year's Eve and then during the day yesterday."

"Next of kin?"

"Her husband Neil works at a law firm in Atlanta. It should be easy to find him. I can reach out and let him know what happened if you'd prefer," Eve offered.

My friend, Officer Blaire, appeared on the scene. Darnell directed her to go to Mrs. Turner's room at the Fulton Inn and ask if anyone saw her leaving the hotel late last night and if there seemed to be anything unusual about her movements.

"This happened last night?" I asked. "She didn't drown this morning?"

"Correct. The medical examiner, Diane Evans, was contacted and should be here shortly to confirm that. But to me, it's pretty obvious that this happened several hours ago. Her clothing was soaked at some point and has been drying in the morning sun."

Behind us, Peaches gagged when she heard that. Loretta kneeled and put her arms around her.

"Do you know of any reason why she would have come out here last night?" Darnell asked.

"I certainly don't," Eve said. We were to get together here this morning. Chris probably mentioned we were going to spread Linda's ashes."

"Yes, ma'am, he did. I'll need to talk to you ladies more," Darnell said, "But if you'd like to leave, you can go ahead now."

"If it's okay, we'd prefer to stay with our friend until they take the body away," Eve said. "We came this morning to memorialize Linda, and now the Secret Sisters have lost another member to this river. It doesn't seem right to just turn our backs on her at this time."

Darnell was making notes but paused. "What did you mean by that? Who are the Secret Sisters, and what was that about losing a second friend to the river?"

While Eve explained the drowning of Matilda East-wood to Darnell, Jackie stood to one side and walked as close to the shoreline as the police officers allowed. She seemed absorbed in taking in details of the landscape. Chris kept to himself at the water's edge. Ella had joined Peaches on the grassy bank. Their conversation was a soft blur of sound amidst the quietly lapping water. Loretta, too, had moved away from her friends. She stood with arms crossed, looking out over the river.

I tried to imagine how this place had looked forty years ago. How lovely it must have been for them. Bonfire Beach. Teens on blankets. Laughing. Horsing around. Jumping into the river, then bobbing up, shaking off the water. Young innocent lives. The future ahead. And no knowledge of what that future held.

Jackie rejoined me and introduced herself to Darnell. "Paddy Murphy took me out in his fishing boat to photograph the river. We went through this area late last night. I remember turning around at Shaw's, upriver from here. So, I know we passed by this pier twice. I took videos on my phone for location bearings of the stills I snapped. I could search and see if anything shows up on either of those formats."

"I'd appreciate that. I always welcome information from the public," Darnell said. "May I ask how you know Paddy?"

"He served as a police officer and then as chief of police in my hometown of Harmony," Jackie said.

"He's a good friend of mine. I respect and appreciate his understanding of human behavior and logical approach to helping me solve cases. But there is a side to him that I reflect on, and that makes me ask…" Darnell paused, taking off his hat and holding it against his chest. "Why such a lovely lady as you was on the river late at night with that Irish rascal?"

Jackie threw her head back and laughed. "Absolutely innocent, I promise! I'm a photographer, and Paddy was kind enough to take me out to capture the moonlight reflecting on the dark waters. He was a perfect gentleman."

"That's good to hear." Darnell was giving Jackie a card with his contact on it when a heated conversation between Chris and a police officer caught his attention. As Darnell strode toward them, their argument escalated. All of us, even those standing farthest away, turned our heads to listen in on what was being said.

Chris had his face up close to the officer's, getting more agitated by the minute. "Just because someone drowned here? I'm trying to fulfill my mother's wishes and can't stay in this town forever while you try to figure out what happened."

Darnell stepped in. "Sir, step back from the officer,

and please lower your voice. This might not have been an accidental drowning, and we'd like to keep the scene intact until the cause of death is determined. Additionally, Mr. Pratt, we'll need to talk further with you. So please don't leave the area without notifying me."

Chris was not happy. With a huff, he stormed toward the three Secret Sisters still here. "I suppose you all heard that. I had plans to stay here tonight, anyway. Now I guess I have no choice. Look, I'm sorry you all just lost your friend…"

"And we're sorry you lost your mother, Chris. But there's nothing any of us can do about it now," Eve said.

Chris suddenly slumped and let out a quick breath. "Guess you're right. But now I have no idea what the outcome of all this will be." He grabbed a small duffle that rested against a nearby tree and pulled three small packages out of it. "But here are the packets that Mom put together for you."

"Will you spread her ashes here today?" Loretta asked.

"It's just so frustrating. I don't know what I'm going to do right now. I guess go back to the lodge and go fishing. I might just do the deed by myself once the police clear out."

"We'd be happy to be with you through this difficult

time, Chris," Peaches said. "We loved your mom so much."

"I did too. Let me think about it. I'll be in touch." And he turned to walk away, passing by the medical examiner as she arrived on the scene.

CHAPTER SEVEN

I gave a brief nod to Dr. Diane Evans as she walked past me, heading toward the location of the body. Jesse was walking alongside her. "Hey Katie," he called out, "I thought I recognized your golf cart. What brings you here?"

"I could say the same for you," I replied with a small smile.

"I was on my way to town to buy some supplies for the fishermen at my lodge and noticed all the emergency vehicles parked in the turnoff." Jesse gestured toward Chris. "Hey, that guy that just passed is staying at Shaw's. Said he was here for a fishing trip but didn't come very well prepared. I set him up with some loaner gear we have and rented him a small fishing boat. What's up with the guy?"

"He discovered the body," I said motioning toward the pier. "I'm here because I was coming back from Ella's when we heard the sirens. She said I had to stop because something bad is happening to someone I know."

"Ella has a certain insight…no, that's not quite it." Jesse rubbed his face and stared down at the ground as though the words he was searching for were written in the sand at our feet. "Perhaps a heightened sensitivity to things. I'm struggling to find the right words. But back to the point, Ella said you knew the victim?"

"I don't think the victim is who Ella meant. Her words were present tense…something bad is happening. Betty Jo died hours ago." I explained who Betty Jo was and why Eve, Loretta, Peaches, and Chris were gathered here this morning.

Jesse nodded. "I get it now. The bad thing happening was the sorrow your friends were experiencing."

"Right, something like that," I answered, still confused by everything going on around me. I was glad we'd stopped, but now it was time to continue on my way back to Seaside. I knew I would talk with Eve, Loretta and Peaches later when things had settled down. "I've got to go. Can you believe it? Our reclusive friend Ella has agreed to go on a boating jaunt with some friends of mine. I want to get her back to town before she changes her mind."

"I'll walk out with you. Let me just talk to Darnell and let him know I'll help in any way I can. Diane mentioned that the officer who called her said this could be a suspicious death. Think that Chris had anything to do with it?"

"Honestly, I hadn't even considered that possibility, Jesse," I answered. The thought of it seemed improbable. What motive would he have? But then who would have wanted Betty Jo dead? It had to be an awful accident.

When Loretta heard I was leaving, she asked if there was room on my golf cart for her to ride, adding that since Chris left before doing what they came here for, to spread Linda's ashes, she didn't want to stay. Eve and Peaches looked surprised but didn't say anything to encourage her to stay.

"Sure. The small rear seat seats two, but the uphol- stery is a little cracked from the sun. If you don't mind that, you can sit back there next to Ella," I said. "Are you sure you don't want to ride back with Eve and Peaches?"

Loretta shook her head, and without another word, she started walking alone on the footpath that led to the road.

Eve's lips pursed in frustration while Peaches eyes were brimming with tears again.

"Are you two going to be okay here?" I asked them.

"We'll stay with Betty Jo until they take her body away." Eve reached for Peaches hand. "And we'll wait on doing anything more until Chris decides how he wants to handle spreading the ashes. It's up to him."

Diane Evans was still examining the body but smiled and waved toward Jesse as he finished talking to Darnell. I'd run into her at the McCracken Mansion when Paul McCracken's body was found. But that was in the dark of night. Seeing her in this bright morning sunlight, she looked kind of young to be a doctor. According to Blaire, she had just recently begun and was new to the department and lots of the younger officers had already learned she wasn't married.

"That was nice of you to talk to Darnell and offer help. He's so good about accepting help from all sources," I said as we turned to follow Ella and Jackie out.

"Agreed. He's willing to ask the extra questions and admit what he doesn't know. Diane found some unusual marks but is withholding a definitive answer as to cause of death until she can do a thorough exam. So sad." Jesse stopped, taking my arm to hold me back so we weren't overheard. "Look, Katie, while I have you alone, I wanted to say that I hoped you didn't mind me sneaking that New Year's Eve kiss."

He looked uncertain. Shy. It was kind of sweet. But I restrained myself. Did I mind the kiss? Not at all. In fact, I enjoyed it much more than I thought I would. But not good to move too fast, to seem too eager. Jesse had to know that I found him attractive. I was sure many other women did, including the beautiful new doctor.

"No problem at all," I replied, trying to sound casual. "There was a lot of kissing happening that night."

Jesse's face broke into a smile, revealing a dimple on his left cheek. He took a step closer, his hand reaching to tuck a loose strand of hair behind my ear. "Well, I enjoyed it," he said, his voice low and husky.

* * *

On the ride back to town, I drove slowly because of my two rear passengers. I didn't need either one of them bouncing off. And also, because I wanted time to savor Jesse's comment. I enjoyed the idea that he liked the kiss, but was I ready for a romantic relationship? Honestly, tempting as it was, I had to say no. Not yet.

"Who was that handsome young man you were talking to on the beach?" Jackie asked.

"Jesse Shaw. His family owns the fishing lodge nearby. And he's the one who introduced me to Ella."

"Seemed like a nice person. Are you two dating?"

That question caught me off guard. "No, I'm not dating someone anytime soon. The guy I left behind in LA soured me on men."

Out of the corner of my eye I caught the grin on Jackie's face. "It looked like Jesse would be sweet enough to take away that sour taste."

Time for a change of subject. "Think you'll find any helpful information on your camera?"

"I'm sure going to try," Jackie said. "I used to do crime scene photography when I was starting out. But it's been so long since I've involved myself in a murder situation."

Ella and Loretta were in the rear-facing seat, so the wind muffled their conversation as we drove along on River Road. From what I could make out, Ella was trying to comfort Loretta about her loss of Betty Jo. I heard Ella mention Tilly's name but couldn't hear Loretta's response. My sense was that Loretta just wanted to get back home. The morning had taken a toll on her.

After dropping Loretta off at her house, I drove to the marina, where Scott, Sophia, and Jack were waiting for Ella and Jackie to arrive. While they were getting organized, I asked Ella how she knew about Tilly.

"Her family and mine were neighbors. She was younger than me, so I knew her sister Frankie a little better. But she was one of my early guinea pigs when I started studying tarot." Ella gasped and quickly covered her mouth. "Is that bad to say? Understand I was a novice then. Looking back, I jumped into the practice pretty quickly and quite unqualified."

"I'll bet you've refined your skills since then. You're a very perceptive woman."

"Thank you. I'll take that as a compliment. But the reason I knew about Tilly was because her death coincided with the time when my home burned down." Ella took a deep breath before continuing, "I lost everything in the fire and moved into my parents' old farm home. I became much more introspective and more attuned to my intuition during those long, lonely days. More deeply aware of surrounding energies."

Jackie overheard us and said, "Oh, I'm so sorry to hear you had a house fire. That must have been very upsetting."

I cringed. Upsetting was a mild word for what Ella had gone through, but Jackie didn't know the entire tragic story about losing her husband and children.

Ella took it in stride—she probably was used to people extending sympathy—and simply said, "Yes, it was."

"What happened?" Jackie asked.

"Locals thought the fire could have been caused by sparks from our old wooden cooking stove or a lightning strike during the storm we had that night. However, I had my own suspicions. My husband had recently confronted poachers on our land, and I couldn't help but wonder if they were behind the blaze."

"Still, what a shock. But you've created such an oasis of calm and serenity to live in now," Jackie said. "I've never had my cards read. If you still do that, I'd be interested in getting a reading sometime."

"I do. I'd be delighted to read your cards, Jackie," Ella said. "It would offer me the means to thank you for doing this for me."

"We're ready to take off," Jack called out and reached for Ella's hand to help her on board *Sophia's Dream.*

I watched as the group left the marina and went south toward the open waters of the cove. They'd head east to enjoy the wildlife refuge on St. John Island, escaping into a wilderness where nature ran the show.

CHAPTER EIGHT

My next stop was at Kenmare Cottage to pick up the star fruit and strawberry jam Maeve had canned for me.

Maeve and Winnie's backsides were the first thing that caught my eye. The path they'd been working on must have hit a roadblock. They were both bent over a gnarly mess of weeds and branches, determined to conquer the unruly shrubbery.

Maeve leaned back on her haunches, tipping her head side-to-side to assess their progress, while Winnie bent down and used her knuckles to push herself up from the ground with a satisfied grunt.

"Was going to ask if you needed help," I called out.

"Lordy girl, don't give us a startle like that," Winnie grumbled, removing her gardening gloves to brush the dirt from her hands and bib overalls.

"Katie! What a pleasant surprise." Maeve reached up for my hand. "I'll take that offer of help. Should have brought out my stool."

"Looks like you two are making progress on the path." There had to be a good twenty feet of vegetation between the cottages here. Raven climbed atop the bags of mulch that were stacked to one side, waiting for the time they could be spread on the footpath.

"Perfect time for a break. It'll be real nice when I don't have to take that long walk 'round the sidewalk jus' to come see Maeve or fumble my way through them pesky branches," Winnie said.

"I agree. We could use a rest. How about joining us for some sweet tea, Katie?"

"I would love to. And I wanted to pick up that jam you promised me."

"Oh, right. Yes," Maeve said. "You two sit out here on the porch while Raven and I go get our tea and your jars of jam."

I smiled. Raven was happily following Maeve, knowing there would be treats inside. The wicker chair Winnie chose made soft, melodic creaks and pops as it adjusted to her weight, while the chains supporting my porch swing added rhythmic squeaks. Green grass surrounded by a white picket fence separated us from the street, creating an oasis I was more than willing to sink into after this morning's events. This might be a good time to pick Winnie's brain.

"Winnie, I'm glad you're here. You know this town and its history. Maybe you'd be willing to shed some light on a few things that have come to my attention in the past two days."

"You know me, I'm a regular flashlight 'bout stuff," Winnie said.

Where to start? It seemed surreal that the body of a woman lay dead among the river grasses rippling under the old fishing pier just miles from where we sat on the porch of this cottage. I decided to start by briefly explaining what had happened this morning.

Winnie couldn't recall Betty Jo. "That's way too long ago for this old lady. You say her body was found by some old fishing pier just out of town, and before you get to Shaw's? I remember a young teen dying some-where around there decades ago."

"That would probably be Matilda Eastwood," I said. "She was one of a group of girls that called themselves the Secret Sisters. Peaches, Loretta, and Eve were part of the group. Linda Pratt was, too, and she died just recently. They were gathering with her son Chris to spread her ashes at Bonfire Beach."

Maeve pushed through the screen door with our iced sweet tea and a tray of soft biscuits with jam, Raven prancing behind her, sharply twitching her tail to avoid it getting caught in the closing door. "At our last book club, I overheard Eve and Peaches talking about someone who passed away. Is this the woman you just mentioned?" Maeve asked.

"Right. That was Linda. It was her ashes they spread at the high school football field and on the beach at Horseshoe Island yesterday," I said, reaching for a biscuit. "And this morning, they were all meeting at the old swimming hole and pier they'd spent so much time at, too."

"Now I understand. Those must have been places where Linda had good memories from growing up," Maeve said. "What a nice thing for her son to do. I don't get why she didn't just get a plot in the cemetery here but to each his own."

"So, you're telling me two gals from that group died in the same place? That Bonfire Beach spot you was at this morning." Winnie made the sign of the cross over her ample bosom. "Those dang high school kids always messing around back then. Kind of a scandal what happened to that young girl. Boyfriend charged if I remember right."

Maeve passed me a glass of tea, asking, "Why were you there though?"

"I was bringing Ella back to town because Jackie

invited her out on a boat ride with the Daniels. We heard the sirens, so we went to investigate. The ladies were all gathered at Bonfire Beach this morning to meet Chris and spread the last of Linda's ashes. Chris found Betty Jo's body."

"Suppose Ella got one of her visions about it," Winnie snarked. "She's a strange one."

"Why do you think so?" Maeve asked in a slightly annoyed tone. She must have gotten tired of Winnie implying Ella was odd in some way. "Sure, she's a loner, but when you get to know her, she's a pleasant, friendly and engaging person. I think she's becoming more and more social as time goes on. Just look at her going out on a boat for the afternoon with four people she doesn't even know."

"Suppose you're right about that, but I'm entitled to my truth. Isn't that what young ones say now?" Winnie replied, staring at me as though daring me to confront her too.

"Winnie, just out of curiosity, could you tell me what you know about that time when Tilly died?" I asked.

"Well, the boyfriend was meeting her after she got done with waitressing at the fishing lodge's restaurant. He found her dead, figured she drowned, and he tried CPR, but it didn't work. She was dead. He runs out to his car parked on the road to go and find help."

"Poor thing. She drowned at the beach where they hung out," Maeve said.

"Nope. That's what they all thought at first, but I learned from Betty Jo that it wasn't an accidental drowning, and the police ended up charging her boyfriend, Jimmy," I said.

"But why would her boyfriend hurt her?" Maeve asked.

"I 'member. The autopsy found she was pregnant. Maybe that young boyfriend didn't want a kid, and they argued. Arguments can end up with someone falling or getting pushed…" Winnie let the words trail off ominously.

"So, he went to jail?" Maeve asked.

"Oh no. Got off scot-free. No real proof. Just circumstantial evidence, they said. I recall the kid had a good reputation around town. He had that charm of the star quarterback of the state title-winning team about him. But that image sure got dragged through the mud during those days." Winnie stood up and stretched. "Enough talk for me. I gotta clean up from this morning's work. Have a shift at the hospital coffee shop. You'd be right proud of me and my barista skills."

"Can I ask you two one more quick thing? From what I observed, Betty Jo's return to Seaside Cove appeared to agitate Loretta to no end. At the Coffee

Corner yesterday morning, she told me she was tempted to strangle Betty Jo."

"What on earth made her say that?" Maeve asked.

"From the little I saw of Betty Jo, she seemed very opinionated and with a touch of narcissism to boot. I get that part of her being annoying for Loretta. But then, today, she asked to ride back to town with me, even after Eve and Peaches decided to stay until the body was removed. That seemed pretty cold. I mean, the woman was dead."

"That certainly don't sound like the Loretta I know. I got no idea what might have gotten into her, but let me think on it, Katie," Winnie said as she turned to walk down the porch steps. "Thanks for the tea, Maeve. I gotta go home and finish up *The Women* for tomorrow's meeting."

"Katie, what you said about Loretta is bothering me. I hope she doesn't blame herself for having negative thoughts about Betty Jo. And then to discover her dead like that. It could really weigh on a person's conscience," Maeve said as she tidied up the porch. "I hope no one overheard what she told you."

"Me too."

CHAPTER NINE

After the day I'd had, I fully planned to kick back and watch the sunset from my balcony. But as I pulled up to the house and began to climb the stairs to my second-floor apartment, Aubrey caught up with me. "Hey friend, want to share a bottle of wine with me?" she asked. The bottle of wine she held in her hand assured me she honestly wanted to have a sit and sip as we had taken to calling these moments, whether coffee in the morning or drinks at night.

"Perfect! Come on up," I said, stepping out of the golf cart. Raven knocked a jar of jam off the seat as she pushed her way past me. "Hey you, chill!"

"She's ready for a sit and sip, too," Aubrey said as she grabbed the jar before it hit the ground. "Don't you think it's time to treat yourself to a new golf cart? Something not quite so barebones and old as this model. Maybe a cute color and with some storage compartments for jam?"

She had a point. I'd bought this cart second-hand, thinking I wouldn't use it much. But boy, was I mistaken. I rarely took my car out anymore. "I know. I just haven't taken the time. Have you been at your desk all day?"

"Yes, and I could regale you with tales of my mundane day, but truth be told, I would rather just bask in the happiness of surviving yet another hump day and gratitude for being done with it," Aubrey said.

"Then you probably haven't heard about what happened on the river."

"You're so right! Nose to the grindstone all day long... but with a glass of wine and this glorious sunset, I'm ready for a juicy river tale. Tell me. News of a record catfish catch?"

"Ah, no. Not that sort of story, but if you're up for it, I'll share my whirl of a day, including the river incident."

Raven chose Aubrey's lap to curl up on as we settled in on my balcony. I poured our wines, and we toasted to another beautiful Florida sunset.

"And to friendships and felines," Aubrey added before taking a sip of her wine and relaxing back into the floral cushion with a sigh. "Okay. Ready for the story."

"Friendship is where I'll start," I said. "You know Evelyn Brooks, right?"

"Sure. Remember, she helped with the haunted mansion last Halloween? Plus, she's kind of a neighbor. I don't know her like you do," Aubrey said, tipping her nose up in the air. "I'm not in that highbrow book club sort of society."

"I could sneak you into some of our exclusive events. We have a club meeting tomorrow night."

"Ah. No thanks," Aubrey said. "But get on with your story."

"You don't know what you're missing," I teased. "Well anyway, you also know Loretta Quinn and Peaches Kershaw. They, along with three other women, formed a group in high school called the Secret Sisters."

"Auld Lang Syne and all that," Aubrey sang, stroking Raven, who responded with a long, soft purr. "I have my group of friends here and some of us have been together since our ancient auld days of high school. But hard to imagine still sticking together for what...like centuries?"

"Not centuries, but decades for sure. And they aren't exactly together anymore. One of them, Tilly, passed away a couple of years out of school. A second one, Linda Pratt, died recently," I said. "And a third member of the Secret Sisters, Betty Jo Turner, was in town for the memorial gathering for their lost sister, Linda."

"So go on. What does this have to do with the river? Hold on!" Aubrey tapped her finger alongside her forehead. "Let me guess. Linda's ashes were scattered on the river in a tribute to their sisterhood because they all loved to fish, and she alone held the biggest catfish on record until..."

"Not exactly, but you're right about one thing. The ash-spreading event was real but did not involve a fishing record. Betty Jo, the one who came in from Atlanta, was found dead this morning by the river."

Aubrey's jaw dropped, her eyes widening in disbelief. "No way," she gasped. "Me and my flippant remark. I had no idea this was what you were leading up to. So, this Betty Jo person came to town, and now she's dead, too? How sad for them all. What happened to her?"

"They, the sisters and Linda's son had spread her ashes at the high school football field and the beach on Horseshoe Island yesterday. All spots where happy memories were made. The third and final place was to be at an old pier and swimming beach on the river called Bonfire Beach."

"She died there near the river they loved? Gosh, hard to imagine."

"And extra emotional because it was the very place their friend Tilly drowned decades ago."

"What? That's crazy!" Aubrey set her glass down and leaned forward intently. Raven was startled off her lap and hissed her dissatisfaction. "But how does this tie in with your day?"

"I was on River Road and saw the emergency vehicles pull over. I followed the paramedics and police walking on a trail through the woods and down to the river's edge."

"Where they found her body?" Aubrey asked.

I nodded and poured us both more wine before going on, telling her about who was there and how everyone was reacting.

"You have had an entirely different day than me," Aubrey said. "This is quite a story. So did this woman drown, too?"

"It's up in the air at this point. Most likely, but the medical examiner will let Darnell know soon."

"The same spot, you say. Is that swimming hole and fishing pier still in use?" Aubrey asked, her brow furrowing in concentration.

"Didn't look like it. The boards on the pier were peeling and warped, and moss was covering the roof of the decrepit fishing shack. Plus, didn't look like a fire had burned in that fire pit for many years."

"Do you remember those old papers your Uncle Paddy found behind the wall at the pub? The ones I wanted to check out before giving them to the historical society?"

"Sure. And I recognize that twinkle in your eye. I'm thinking you are making some kind of connection."

"Well, my friend, I do believe I am making one," Aubrey said. "I think I may have some newspapers that covered the tragedy of Miss Tilly's sad demise. Mind you, hers wasn't the story that first caught my eye. A photograph of the charred remains of a house with the headline that two children and their father perished in the blaze. I remember you telling me about Ella Winchester, so I pulled out those papers to show them to you. But anyway, that's where I saw the stories about a former cheerleader's body being found."

"Wow. I'd like to see those papers! In fact, Ella was with me today. Can you get those specific papers out?"

"Tonight?" Aubrey asked with a surprised expression.

"Why not? Aren't you the seize-the-moment sort of friend? Raven and I could go down to your place right now."

Aubrey tilted her head and flashed a wide grin before grabbing the almost empty bottle of wine. I picked up our two wine glasses, and Raven followed us down the staircase to the first floor.

Darkness arrived, and Aubrey switched on the light as we entered her formal dining room. She headed to a corner of the room, where a box holding old newspapers sat. It was guarded by a three-foot-tall stone gargoyle, apparently an oddity collected by Aubrey's great-aunt. A world traveler, her home had become a museum to showcase her souvenirs. When Aubrey inherited the home, the collection came along with it.

"Sit. Sit." Aubrey directed me as she plopped down on the floor next to the box. A musty odor rose from the box as she began to rifle through papers, setting some on the floor next to her.

Raven, meanwhile, had climbed onto the gargoyle's shoulders and peered down on what Aubrey was doing.

"Raven, get down," I scolded.

"She's fine. That stone is indestructible," Aubrey said. "If it survived the elements for over three hundred years on a church in England, a kitty sitting on it is not going to matter."

Raven gave me a haughty look, and I responded by sticking my tongue out at her.

"Here's the newspaper with a photograph of the fire-damaged house on the front page." Aubrey handed me a yellowed newspaper.

I hesitated to open it, afraid the dry, brittle paper might disintegrate in my hand. Carefully, I unfolded the old paper to reveal the front page spread, a grainy photo of the remains of the Winchester home.

As I began to read the article about the tragedy, she placed three more issues next to me and said, "Could you quickly skim through these newspapers? I'm pretty sure one of them has a story about the drowning. Once we find it, I can narrow down our search by dates."

Aubrey didn't hesitate to rummage willy-nilly through the papers, so I followed suit, handling them less delicately as she muttered, "It would have been easier if I had put these in chronological order the first time."

I was in the third paper when I found what we were looking for. "Eureka! I found it! Look, here's even a picture of her."

The formal, posed photograph looked like it was taken from Tilly's high school yearbook. Her long, wavy hair cascaded over one shoulder, with bangs framing her bright eyes and expressive smile. The caption below the photo read *Matilda Eastwood drowned at Bonfire Beach, a popular teenage hangout.*

After opening a fresh bottle of wine, we began to put the newspapers in order by date and discovered that the autopsy revealed she'd suffered a blow to the head that killed her before her body entered the water. It was also revealed that she was in the early months of a pregnancy. This treasure trove of information spread out before us was as though we had opened a time capsule and were watching the case unfold in real-time. And it agreed with what Winnie remembered about that time too. Another high school photograph showed up, this time of one James Conrad. He was identified as a former local high school quarterback standout who was being charged with the murder.

"Maybe a love triangle?" Aubrey asked. "That's always good for a crime of passion. Or unrequited love?"

Raven was now fast asleep, on top of the gargoyle's shoulders, her paws dangling down as though hugging the beast.

"How random that of all the old papers were there and not thrown away," I said.

"Right, very cool. Didn't they do stuff like putting paper in the wall for insulation or as a sound barrier? We should ask little Mr. Green," Aubrey said. "Who knows, maybe it was to muffle the sound of their wild children while a funeral was going on downstairs and people were grieving. That must have been a weird upbringing."

We read quotes from friends of the deceased. I pointed out that most of these were from the group of Secret Sisters. Then Aubrey found photographs of Jimmy's parents and Tilly's parents and sister leaving the courthouse during the trial. *Local families torn apart by trial as it moves into week three.* Then in big, bold headlines, *James Conrad acquitted and fear of a murderer on the loose spreads through Seaside Cove.*

"So, they never solved the case?" Aubrey murmured. "Wow. How hard for everyone."

"That's what I was told. Sounds like he was the only guy they really went after. Here's a statement from the police chief." I read aloud, *"We did a thorough investigation, and I'm confident we had our man, but a jury of his peers decided otherwise. Someone got away with murder. No further comment at this time."*

A shiver ran through me. The history of that lonely spot on the river affected me deeply. I couldn't even begin to imagine how the Secret Sisters must have felt when they returned there today. They must have mentally prepared themselves to say goodbye to their dear friend as her ashes were scattered over this spot where they'd had such youthful fun years ago. But instead, they were confronted with another dead body lying in the same spot where a friend's body had been found decades ago. I wondered what memories resurfaced for each of them by that shocking sight. The more I read, the more the case of Matilda Eastwood's death piqued my interest. Two cases so interconnected in real life but separated by time.

"What the heck! Let's go for it," Aubrey said. "I'm all in if you want to try to solve this cold case."

"Aubrey, my thoughts exactly. Because seeing that abandoned Bonfire Beach today did something to me. The memories that are buried there are unfathomable."

"It's calling for us to don our detective caps, isn't it?" Aubrey paused dramatically, holding up the empty bottle. "Or is it just the wine whispering sweet nothings?"

"Oh, my friend, the wine always has something important to say," I chipped in. "But yes, let's solve this mystery together."

"Excellent idea. We'll be partners in crime-solving," Aubrey exclaimed. "I'll take charge of organizing these articles while you track down that elusive reporter who wrote all the articles we just read. Together, we are the unstoppable duo, and with some hard work and a sprinkle of luck, we'll crack this case wide open."

CHAPTER TEN

The next morning, I made a beeline for the Cove Gazette to talk with Hannah Brooks, the owner, editor, and head reporter. Hannah's family, the Nelsons, had founded the paper, and it now had twice weekly editions and a daily online presence.

She welcomed me with unexpected enthusiasm. "I'm so glad you stopped by! It feels like it's been forever since we've caught up. I don't think I've seen you since last year."

"No, I just saw you last…very funny. That's right, it was last year!"

"Such wittiness is but one of the reasons I became a reporter. People love clever stories with timely twists." Hannah cleared her throat. "I love to do that to friends every January. My small pleasure. Now, to what do I owe this visit?"

"I'd like to know if…" But before I could finish my question, Hannah's daughter, Officer Blaire, showed up. She gave her mom a peck on the cheek and said, "Hey Katie, how are you doing? Sorry about yesterday. I could see how hard it was for you and your friends."

"More for them because they were expecting one sad thing, which was hard enough, but that was usurped by something much worse. Hope you find out who did this awful thing."

"We're still investigating. In fact, Mom, I stopped in because Darnell asked me to let you know that the medical examiner has confirmed this was not a drowning. There was no water in her lungs. Dr. Evans said she died from a blow to the head and neck area. He thought the public should be notified. He'd like the usual comments about if anyone has information that might help the police to call the department."

"Of course," Hannah said. "I'll put the new information in the online edition."

As I processed the details of what I'd just heard, it became increasingly clear to me how much this resembled Tilly's murder. At first, both appeared to be a simple drowning but ended up being murders. "Hannah," I said, trying to wrap my head around the eerie similarities. "Do you realize this is almost identical to a case from over four decades ago? The victim was a teenager, and she died in the same spot and manner."

"Whoa, that's spooky." Blaire moved to grab a water bottle from the small fridge kept in the corner of the office. "Did you know that, Mom?"

"I can't recall it. Might be an interesting angle to the current story." Hannah reached for a pencil and notepad. "What was her name, and how did you know about this, Katie?"

The words spilled out of me, explaining Tilly's story as reported over forty years ago. With the little knowledge I had, I explained how the two murders were linked through the Secret Sisters group. Even as I was telling it I realized how good it felt to put the information I had into words and in such a way that Blaire and Hannah could grasp. They both seemed to understand where I was coming from. But were Aubrey and I getting over-excited about something that might be too difficult to tackle?

"Are you saying both murders are somehow connected?" Blaire asked.

"Only in that they involve the same small group of women and occurred at the same location. I'm focused on this cold case. It just drew me in, maybe because I've gotten to know some players from the past, and I stood on the spot it happened. And I mean, come on, what's the likelihood of there being any connection to yester-day's murder? It's just some weird, out-of-this-world phenomenon or something."

"Cosmic coincidence or emotional convergence kind of thing?" Blaire asked.

"Wow! That's quite a mouthful. I'll try and remember what you said. Aubrey will love how you put it!"

Blaire fist-bumped me. "Us police are deeper than we look."

"I'll be honest," Hannah said. "Having those papers is priceless. We didn't even do microfiche back then. It was an added expense my father didn't want to take on. We kept copies of every paper, but a terrible flood from a hurricane that went through the Gulf Coast destroyed most of them. You say she's taking them to the Histor-ical Society? Maybe that's not the best place. The library might be better to archive them."

"I could have Aubrey email you a copy of the articles. She's scanning them for us," I offered. "Are you familiar with a reporter named Vincent Pahlke? It was his byline on the murder articles we read last night."

"Yes, he's still around. He lives in the mobile home park on the northwest side of town. He'll stop by occa-sionally to chat about things. I don't think I have a phone number for him, but I'm sure if you go to the Palm Gardens office, the manager can help you find him. But why are you getting so involved with this, Katie? You could just hand this information over to Darnell."

"It's not anything new yet. We don't have any new solid leads." I shrugged. "And now, it seems kind of silly in the light of day. But we thought the recollections of individuals connected to that old case might have improved over time."

"Back to the present. I met the victim's husband, Neil Turner, earlier this morning. He came in to have me help him write an obituary for his wife. He was still in a daze. We ended up sitting together and having a cup of coffee as we worked on the obituary. I think he needed someone to talk to and process what had happened."

"I'm glad you met him," I said. "It sounded like his wife didn't see much of her old friends over the years."

"He's planning to return to Atlanta in a couple of days and hopes to meet the other sisters before he leaves. I suggested Paddy's Pub," Hannah said.

"Hey, thanks for the recommendation," I said.

"My pleasure. Neil said his next stop was the Green Funeral parlor to deal with handling his wife's body. Then he would check in with Darnell. Poor guy. A lot on his plate."

"Does Darnell have any person of interest or suspect?" I asked Blaire.

"I guess you'd call Chris Pratt a person of interest. Darnell talked with him at the site Wednesday morning and then had him come in for an interview that afternoon. Apparently, he and Betty Jo met in the bar in Shaw's Lodge on Tuesday night. She had gone there to talk with him, but arrived pretty wasted, was how he put it. Then things turned confrontational with some of the other patrons. She eventually left, still under the influence of alcohol."

"So, might she have been drunk, knocked her head on something, and fallen in the river?" Hannah asked.

"He's considering all possibilities, but based on the location of the blow to her neck, it doesn't seem like a fall. And then there still is the question of what she was even doing there that time of night," Blaire said. "Today, Darnell is going out to talk to Jesse and his staff and find out if anyone saw her or had any other information. Gotta get back to work. Thanks for the water, Mom."

Hannah bit her lower lip, tapping her pencil on the pad in front of her. "Hold on a second. I have an idea. Blaire, would the police have a case file for that murder?"

"I can check," Blaire answered. "The station moved a few years ago, and I know they purged a lot of records. But it's a possibility. Since the case was never solved, it's highly likely the evidence files would have been kept. I'll contact you guys later."

"Why didn't I think of that? It would be perfect if there were more than the newspaper articles," I said. "But right now, I'm off to see if I can find Mr. Vincent Pahlke. See you later tonight at the book club meeting."

CHAPTER ELEVEN

The houses in this part of town were far from the river and the cove, and they seemed to lack any cooling breeze from the Gulf. Unlike the neat rows of charming cottages in Maeve's neighborhood or the grand mansions where Hannah and Greg lived with Eve Brooks, these homes were much smaller and not as well-maintained. Faded plastic children's toys, deflated blowup pools, and child-sized bicycles littered the yards.

But as I turned in on a crushed shell driveway, it was clear that the Palm Gardens mobile home park was well taken care of. There were no untrimmed grass areas or poorly tended flower beds in sight. Each unit had its own small concrete patio with neatly arranged outdoor furniture and potted plants.

The manager's office was locked, and no one

answered my pounding on the door. I tried the phone number posted to call in case of an emergency, but it was no longer in service. Cupping my hands around my eyes, I peered through the glass but couldn't see anyone. Now what?

Getting back into my golf cart, I made my way slowly through the park. It was huge! Where most streets in Seaside Cove were either numbered or named after aquatic birds, here they went with seashell names like Conch Court, Cockle Street, and Limpet Lane. The palm trees planted here when it was originally laid out had matured and, like everything else in the landscaping, were well maintained.

Things were generally quiet. I heard an occasional television show or music playing but saw no one outside. Then, I discovered a community center in the middle of all the mobile homes. I parked my cart between one that had a flashy iridescent coat of paint and pink seats and one that was green with gold accents and a Green Bay Packers logo on the hood. Must belong to a Wisconsin snowbird. Maybe Aubrey was right. It might be time for me to upgrade my ride.

The bocce court ahead of me was lined with low palms swaying gently in the breeze, and the men, dressed in T-shirts and shorts, all wearing sun visors or wide-brimmed hats, were deeply engaged in their game.

Their quiet conversations mingled with the occasional clink of bocce balls as they struck against one another. Those waiting their turn rested on benches lining the bocce court, their tanned arms slung across the backrest as they watched the game with keen interest.

I approached the men seated on the bench and asked if any of them knew Vincent Pahlke. Without his eyes leaving the game in front of them, one man spoke. "Who's asking?"

"I'm Katie Murphy and I wanted to ask Mr. Pahlke about some reporting he did long ago. Do you know which home he lives in?"

"Yep," the man answered, glancing up at me, then back to court. "Lives in 35 East Abalone Drive. But he's not home right now."

"Do you have a phone number for him?"

"Not on me."

"Maybe I can just leave a note for him to call me," I suggested.

"You could do that. Or you could just sit down here and wait until the match is over and he can talk to you. That's him right over there in those goofy plaid shorts." The man looked up at me and gave a low chuckle, patting on the bench. "Name is Horace."

I couldn't help but grin. "Why, thank you, Horace. You've been most helpful."

"We aim to please here at Palm Gardens."

It was well worth the wait. Vincent Pahlke, a short, balding man with dark eyes and a gray goatee, had an amazing memory and was more than willing to talk about the Matilda Eastwood murder. He led me to a nearby picnic table set up behind the bocce court benches. I briefly explained who I was and how I ended up here wanting to talk about a murder case from over forty years ago.

Clasping his hands and resting his forearms on the table, he began, "Remember it like it happened last week. That case stuck with me. It was sensational. Such a pretty little thing. Just two years out of high school. Her boyfriend said they were supposed to meet at that old fishing pier the kids called Bonfire Beach after she got off her waitress work at Shaw's Lodge."

"That's what I heard. And he was the one who found her body, right?"

"Yep. Kid was really shaken up. You can only imagine. He claimed he found her and right away ran to the lodge to have them call the police. Course he pulled her up out of the water. But she was already dead," Vincent said.

"My friend and I read your articles last night. But we couldn't find out exactly why they were there that night," I said. "Did you remember anything more about that?"

"The kid claimed Tilly had said she needed to talk with him about something very important. But I couldn't report what it was because he didn't know either." Vincent shrugged his shoulders. "I surmised it might have had something to do with the fact she was pregnant."

"That first came up in the autopsy, right?" I asked as both of us turned to look toward the court, where a loud cheer had gone up. The men were high fiving over winning a match.

"Good job, Horace!" Vincent sent them a fist bump into the air before returning to our conversation. "Jimmy admitted they were having sex, but he said he always used a condom. Didn't say maybe it broke in court, but the lawyer did. Judge had to admonish the audience to keep quiet after a ripple of choked-back laughter and snorts erupted with that testimony."

One guy sitting on the bench burst out laughing. "What the heck. Say it straight, Vincent. The poor kid was getting two-timed."

Another man agreed with him. "Tell her that side of it. Bet she was messing around with another guy and wanted good ole Jimmy to take the blame."

"Obviously, there were lots of opinions and gossip

around town," Vincent said, rolling his eyes. "Some said maybe he asked her to get a backstreet abortion, and she got mad. That they got in a fight, and next thing you know, she falls in and drowns."

"Or, like your friend said, maybe she took on another boyfriend," I suggested.

The two men stepped up to us. "Right, one with more of a future than that big shot quarterback out of school two years and just barely working. You gonna get a sandwich with us Vincent? Or hang here with the cute redhead?"

"Nah, you guys go ahead," Vincent said. "Now, where were we?"

"The town kind of turned against young Jimmy after that," I said. "Even though he was acquitted at the trial. Did you attend the trial?"

"Every day of it."

"What did you think? Was he guilty?" I asked.

"I doubt it." Vincent shrugged. "But no other suspects were ever brought up on charges. Thus, the cold case you are studying."

The men had put the bocce balls in the rack and stopped by again. "There were rumors about some wacko uncle that visited from Georgia. Crazy sorts of things like that. And there was talk about some old rich fisherman who hung around Shaw's. Maybe they had a brief liaison for a good tip."

"Shut up, you stupid old coot, Horace. Tilly wasn't that kind of girl," Vincent snapped before turning back to me. "Sorry about that, miss. Even after this long and with men that old, that foolish talk and those rumors keep popping up."

"And you don't believe she didn't just accidentally drown? Like you said, slip on the wooden pier, hit her head, and fall in?"

"I don't, and not according to the coroner either. Jimmy got off scot-free, but a darkness followed him for the rest of his life. Look, Katie, I'm past due for taking my meds. My home is just down there, a piece. If you have any more questions, you can walk along with me."

I was pleased he was open to more conversation. We left the community center area and started down Abalone Drive. Victor excused himself and went inside his mobile home, returning shortly with a cold bottle of water for me.

"Not fun getting old," he said as he joined me at his patio table. "Now, back to the case."

"You talked about the darkness around Jimmy. Was it because he was guilty? Or was it because that's what most people thought?"

"Good question. Either way, the damage was done. Plus, he lost his girlfriend too. Can't forget that."

"Is he still here in town?" I asked.

"Yes, young lady, he is in the area. Lives a way out. If you are serious about this and not just writing a book or a novel about it, I think I could get him to talk to you. It might take some convincing. So, give me a good reason. The real reason you are doing this. It might be easier to get Jimmy to talk with you."

I told Vincent about Linda and the Secret Sisters. He had memories of the girls, especially Linda, who was a witness at the trial because she was Tilly's roommate. Then I brought up what had happened Tuesday night. Now my interest in the case seemed to make a better connection for him because he admitted he thought of Tilly immediately upon reading about Betty Jo Turner. The last thing I shared was the randomness of Aubrey possessing newspapers from that period of time.

"Interesting," he said with a humph. "My old byline caught your eye, heh? I can see why you are latching on to this."

He also listened intently, nodding slowly as I told him about Frances confronting the group at the football field. "She was very angry and aggressive about the whole thing," I said. "Was she part of your investigative reporting during that time?"

"She was. In fact, she did most of the talking for the family," he said. "Tough young woman. Not the type to soften with age."

"Your reporting seemed to have dismissed the idea that any of Tilly's case could be traced back to someone from Shaw's."

"Always felt something a little off there. But not like Horace said just now. I went there and talked to Hank Shaw. He couldn't come up with any one of the groups they were guiding during that time period that would make trouble for Tilly." Vincent shuffled in his seat. He seemed to be making moves to let me know our conversation was ending.

"Thank you so much for your help," I said. "I'll leave you to your lunch now."

"Katie, here's my phone number. I'd like to see those old papers. Might spark more memories for me," Vincent said. "And I'll reach out to Jimmy to see if he's willing to talk with you. Don't hold your breath, though."

"That would be amazing. Thank you so much. I'll be in touch and arrange for you to see your old newspaper articles. Oh, and I almost forgot, Hannah says hello."

"Keep me in the loop if you would, Katie," he said.

As I walked back to my cart, I turned to wave goodbye. Vincent was staring into the distance as though his mind had returned to the days we'd just been talking about.

CHAPTER TWELVE

We gathered in Eve's luxurious home office once again
for our monthly book club meeting. The crystal chande-
lier hanging from the ceiling cast a warm and inviting
glow over the bookcases that lined the walls and the
plush Persian rugs beneath our feet. From her writing
desk, made of intricately carved cherry wood with a
leather inlay, Eve could take in the view of the cove
through the south-facing windows as she worked. I
chose a seat with the same view so I could watch the
setting sun's reflection on the water as we discussed the
club's latest novel.

With glasses of wine and small plates of appetizers in
hand, the book club ladies settled in to discuss *The
Women* by Kristen Hannah.

The book's exploration of women's often-over-looked roles in history was the first point brought up by Maeve. "I think one of the most powerful things about this book was how the role the women play is often written out of history. Even during such a recent time like the Vietnam War. I was in Ireland during those years, but the way Hannah brought to life the experience of female soldiers was eye-opening."

Winnie let out one of her haughty scoffs. "That war ain't recent, honey. Y'all been losin' track of time. America sent our boys over there, let me think, must be going on over sixty years ago."

It hit home that I was the youngest person in the room. Did I really have anything to contribute to the discussion of an era that I wasn't a part of? I'd give it a try. "It obviously was a different generation than I grew up in, so that could be why, at times, I felt frustrated with her decisions. But then I reminded myself of how young she was when it all began and that there were also so many things changing around her. Wasn't the Vietnam War when reporters first broadcast from active war zones?"

"It was," Hannah answered. "Now anyone can record and broadcast events right to the web from their cell phones."

"What did you all think about how the nurses had to prove themselves over and over, not just to their male counterparts, but to each other?" Eve asked. "Personally, their resilience impressed me."

Everyone agreed on that point. "Many of us still have to keep proving ourselves," Vivian said. "I'm constantly telling myself I can run the Fulton Inn without Marvin. I could never have done what those nurses did. Leave their family behind and travel to a strange country in the middle of a war."

"But then the bonds of sisterhood they forged under those extreme conditions was inspiring," Peaches said. "I admired how they put themselves on the line for each other and became each other's family."

Loretta was idly spinning the antique globe on its brass stand. "That sense of isolation they experienced when they got home got to me. Not being able to talk about what they'd been through. That was heartbreaking." She didn't look up as she continued speaking. "It really showed how hard times affect people mentally as much as physically."

"But the strength she received from her friends was always there," Eve said, giving Loretta a reassuring smile. "Even in the hardest of times."

Was there a signal being sent between them? It made me remember the singing of Auld Lang Syne on New Year's Eve...old times past, long-ago friendships. The value and power they hold.

"I agree with the friendship and support thing, but I thought the love triangle subplot felt unnecessary. Like it was there just to add drama," Marge said.

"A bit of romance always spices things up," Winnie said. "But that triangle thing can get mighty messy. Speaking of messes, can y'all fill us in on what happened to your friend at Bonfire Beach?"

Eve attempted to redirect the conversation back to the book, but after a few minutes, she surrendered, knowing that the recent death would be a topic of great interest for everyone in the room. She recounted the events of the past few days for the rest of us.

"Can you tell us about your conversation with Betty Jo's husband?" Peaches said.

"I was happy I reached him early enough for him to drive down that same day," Eve said. "Of course, he was shaken up, but he said he'd have his secretary clear his calendar immediately so he'd arrive Wednesday night."

"Suppose he has to make arrangements here and all that? He's staying with us at the inn like Betty Jo did," Vivian said.

"I recommended Green's Funeral Home to him. Plus, he wants to put an obituary in a local paper, so I told him about the Cove Gazette for that."

Hannah took up the next part of the story. "He stopped in at the paper's offices on Thursday and we put an obituary together and will coordinate with the Atlanta paper later if he has a memorial there."

"Sounds like he's mighty cold and analytical about it," Winnie drawled as she popped another candied pecan in her mouth. "Gettin' all this organized so quick."

"To be honest, I felt that way too when we hung up," Eve said. "But then he called once he got on the road, wanting to hear more about what had happened. He told me what he knew about his wife's plans for this trip, and then he wanted my perspective on her actions here."

"What an odd way to put it," I said with a shiver. "But maybe it's a lawyer thing."

Eve stood to close an open French door as the evening air had taken on a damp chill. "I think it was an emotional thing. He confided that he was concerned that his wife would be drinking while she was here and that she may have gone to her old sad place."

"Do you think he meant a sad place in her mind or a physical place?" Peaches asked.

"Like Bonfire Beach?" I said. "That could be an explanation or reason for her being at the beach on Tuesday night."

"I thought he meant the beach because he tied it in with her falling in and drowning," Eve answered. "But you could be right, Peaches. Maybe he meant a sad, depressive state of mind."

Loretta shivered. Eve handed her a small throw, but she refused it. Lying the small blanket on the couch within Loretta's reach, Eve continued, "He said she adamantly refused his offer to come here with her for this trip. They spoke on the phone Tuesday night to see how the day went. She told him about where we had scattered the ashes and that one of her friends had upset her. Plus, Linda's son made her anxious. She told him she wasn't joining us for dinner but was thinking about driving around to clear her mind. That was the last time he talked to her."

As Eve spoke, Loretta's face paled. She stood up and placed her glass on an end table with trembling hands. "I'm not feeling well. Sorry, but I think I'd better head home early tonight."

"You look a little under the weather, dear," Vivian said. "I'll walk you home. I'm tired myself."

Despite Loretta's protestations, Vivian insisted on accompanying her out. The two of them left together.

CHAPTER THIRTEEN

Loretta's behavior was out of character. She had been acting oddly for the past few days, but I pushed those thoughts aside as I turned my attention back to the group in front of me. It seemed like a fitting moment to share the project that Aubrey and I had recently taken on together.

"I have some news I'd like to share. You all might find it interesting," I said. "My friend Aubrey and I have become interested in the death of Matilda Eastwood. We're going to open our own investigation into her death."

"Lord help us. Aren't there 'nuff murders to work out without going back forty years to try and solve one?" Winnie asked.

I laughed and shushed her. "Don't worry, the police

will solve Betty Jo's murder in good time. This is something entirely different."

Maeve began nervously wringing her hands. "I don't like the sound of that, Katie. You almost got punched out the last time you put yourself into a murder investigation."

"Auntie, this is not an active case. I don't think I need to fear a crazed killer clown this go-round. The murderer, should we discover him or her, might even be dead at this point."

"How did you two even get this crazy idea in your heads?" Winnie asked. "This still from yesterday when we was sitting on Maeve's porch?"

"It is. When I first heard about Tilly, it was just a sad event from the past. But last night, as I was sharing the story with Aubrey over a glass of wine, she reminded me of an old article she had seen about it. We ended up going to her place and poring through old newspapers together."

"The ones you got from the inside the wall at the pub?" Maeve asked.

"Right, from when the upper deck remodeling started, and they were checking structure issues. Anyway, we read through them and then thought, hey, why not delve deeper and check things out now?"

"Did you find Vincent Pahlke, the reporter you were looking for?" Hannah asked.

"I did, and he was very interested in helping us. He's going to try to get Jimmy, Tilly's boyfriend who was accused and acquitted of her murder, to talk with us. Plus, he suggested we go out to Shaw's River Lodge, where he always felt things could have been more extensively investigated."

"That story became national news." Marge's eyes grew distant, her expression turning somber as she recounted the memory. "During the early years of our marriage, my husband Ken was working full time for his father, Hank. The plan was for him to eventually take over the fishing lodge. Those were busy times. Lots of fishermen come here for the abundance of both freshwater and saltwater fish, and our cabins were often fully booked. Right after they found Tilly's body, curiosity seekers and reporters flocked to us. According to newspaper articles, Matilda Eastwood died after leaving her job as a waitress at Shaw's River Lodge. Her body was found at a nearby pier. We were in their crosshairs. Those articles were sensationalized, almost like the clickbait way of drawing readers' attention now."

"I'll bet Ken remembers those days after the murder. Might he be willing to talk with us?" I asked.

"I think he would. You can usually catch him helping

Jesse during the daytime. Vincent interviewed mainly Hank, but Ken will probably remember him, too."

"Does anyone else have something they'd like to share about that time?"

Eve made her way to a nearby cabinet and swung open its door, retrieving a pile of four books. "If you want to get a sense of the time period, you can flip through my old yearbooks. You'll find Tilly and Jimmy's photos in there. As well as the rest of us old broads."

"Oh, let me see. I haven't looked at mine in years!" Peaches exclaimed. She rapidly flipped through the pages. "Look, here I am in drama class! And here we are in the cheerleading squad."

I leaned in closer behind her, trying to get a better view. The cheer squad was posing for a photo, their huge pompoms held high. Their uniforms were all identical, featuring a large letter S on the tops and pleated skirts with a contrasting color inset. "Which one are you?" I asked, peering at the faces in the picture.

Peaches pointed out herself, Betty Jo, and Tilly. A sudden silence fell upon us as we realized that two of them were no longer with us. Peaches shook her head slightly before drawing our attention to a photo of the squad performing a pyramid. "Tilly used to be on top," she said with a sad smile. "She was a tiny thing."

Hannah had picked up one of the other yearbooks. "I

like to read the inscriptions. Look at this one from Tilly. *Best friends 4ever. Stay cool. Keep quiet.* Ah, what were you supposed to keep quiet about?"

"You don't know everything about me." Eve chuckled. "Don't tell Greg. He might not handle it well."

Hannah laughed at her mother-in-law's remark. "And here I thought Tilly was the wild one of you."

"Tilly could be a little out there at times, but everyone figured she'd settle down with Jimmy, and they'd raise a family right here. I think that idea made her feel stuck sometimes," Eve said. "Anyway, we all sort of drifted apart, going in such different directions after high school. Hey, Peaches, show Katie the photos of Jimmy. He was such a good-looking kid."

The black and white photographs of James Conrad showed a confident, muscular young man. His hair, when it wasn't hidden by a football helmet, was thick and combed back with an attractive natural wave. What would he look like now?

"Can you remember anything about that summer before her murder that would help solve the case?" I asked. "Maybe now, from an adult perspective, things might look different. Clues might mean more than you thought at the time."

Eve went to sit in her desk chair, swiveling to face me. "That was a long time ago. Though I've thought of it often. In fact, in my letter from Linda, she noted one of my books seemed to use a story line similar to our life then. Of all of us, Linda was probably the most attached to the idea of the Secret Sisters."

I'd forgotten about the letters they'd all received from Chris today. "Which book was that again? I'd enjoy reading it."

"She probably meant *Where the Road Ends.* Betty Jo and I were dorm buddies at the University of Florida in Gainesville. It was our second year, and I had a car, so we drove back here together. I remember her saying she was so very ready to find a steady guy to date. And that he sure as heck wasn't going to be found in this small hick town. But that's about typical of Betty Jo. Like Loretta said, she always talked about herself as if she was the most important person in the room. But I will say she found Neil somehow...somewhere, because during our fall semester, she was making plans to transfer to Emory in Atlanta. Her parents were mad about it, but she was adamant. And you know, she didn't talk about the guy much, but she sure had her mind set on him."

"Was that Neil?" Maeve asked.

"Yes, I think he and his family had big standing in Atlanta, and that attracted her," Eve said. "Betty Jo wanted to marry well. To be comfortable. Have the country club lifestyle that Seaside Cove didn't offer."

Peaches closed the yearbook, letting it sit in her lap with her hands resting on top. "I remember going to the beach on Horseshoe Island that summer. We did some barhopping with fake IDs. Tilly was working a couple of jobs then, and Linda was going to summer school, so it was mainly the four of us."

"Weren't there hints of Tilly cheatin' on Jimmy?" Winnie asked. "You know gossip flies in these towns, but I reckon I heard something like that. I do remember folk putting up a screen of dead trees to disguise the path to the pier. Darn goofballs started to take pieces of it."

"I believe that came up in Vincent's coverage of the trial. It made the news, and so curiosity seekers looked for it," I said. "Eve, could I see the letter you got from Linda?"

"Sure, Katie, but it's getting late. I have to work with the notes my editor sent over in the morning. Could we get together tomorrow, say, later in the afternoon?" Eve said as she retrieved a small statue from a shelf behind her desk. The sculpture depicted six dancers in a line, frozen in a moment of movement.

Peaches sighed and walked over to hug her friend. "And now there are three."

CHAPTER FOURTEEN

"Good morning, Winnie," I said as I entered the Coffee Corner. "Is that big box of donuts for the staff at the Humane Society?"

"Well, bless your heart, they ain't for the critters! I was just asking Maeve here if Paddy's Pub would be interested in hosting our Pet Adoption Day for next spring. They usually do it right at the building, but just think about the exposure they'd get here on Main Street."

"Do you think it would work here, though?" Maeve asked Winnie.

"It would be a whole heap more work for us volunteers, but if more animals got homes, that would be great. And maybe we can squeeze some coins out of folks walking by who can't adopt. Guilt is a powerful motivator," Winnie drawled with a mischievous glint in her eye.

"I'm up for it," I said. "I remember you putting the pressure on me when you convinced me to take Raven in. You yourself are a powerful motivator."

Winnie did her laughing snort. "Exactly. Put them cute puppies and kitties out there where folk can see and touch them might be just the thing. I'll let you know how the idea goes over. Catch you later."

Maeve laughed. "Winnie is quite the mover and shaker. But I give her credit for making connections in our little town and donating so much time and effort to the community."

"Morning, ladies," Sophia said as she and her sister-in-law, Jackie Parker, entered our coffee shop. "Umm, it always smells so yummy in here."

"Nice to see you again, Katie," Jackie said. "Another boating day, but just for the boys this time. We're here to pick up coffee and sweet treats for them."

As Sophia and Maeve moved to the bakery display case, Jackie pulled me aside. "Katie, I wanted to let you know that Ella had a marvelous day on Wednesday. She seemed so relaxed and had a huge haul of things for artistic endeavors. She was delighted to find some freshly shred snake skins and lots of unique birds' feathers."

"That's good to hear," I said. "We'll look forward to the new pieces she creates to display for sale here."

"But there is something more I wanted to talk with you about. Two things, actually. First, you won't believe who's joining Jack and Scott for fishing today. Neil Turner! Betty Jo's husband."

"What? How did that come about?"

"He's an attorney in Atlanta and has worked with Jack on some cases. We ran into him here at the pub last night. When Jack asked him what he was doing in Seaside Cove, the poor guy almost broke down right at the bar. Especially when Jack turned to me and asked if that was what I saw Wednesday morning."

"Oh, my gosh. How awkward that must have been," I said. "That was nice of Jack to invite him along fishing today. The guy could probably use a break."

"He was so grateful. He's planning to leave tomorrow, the way it sounds. Hope the guys and the fish provide a needed distraction," Jackie said as I walked with her to help Sophia pick up the coffee cup holder and the box of bakery goods.

"Jackie and I are heading out to the beach to soak up some sun while the guys fish," Sophia said. "Want to join us?"

"Sounds wonderful, but I have plans for the day. Have a good time and don't forget the sunscreen. Oh, and the man who owns Rum Runner on the beach, Tyler Berman, is from Wisconsin. If you end up near his place, please say hello from me."

"And make sure you have a good beach book," Maeve added. "The temperatures will be perfect today."

"Books and Berman, got it," Sophia said.

"Hold on a sec," Jackie said. "The second thing I wanted to let you know was that I think there was evidence on the video and stills I took. I just turned copies over to Darnell. He's upstairs with Paddy looking things over."

"Thanks for letting me know," I said. "Darnell will be glad you got those. Sounds like good information to help the investigation."

Knowing Darnell was upstairs, I decided to go up and see if he would be okay with Blaire getting out the cold case file on Matilda's murder for Aubrey and me.

"I'm good with you looking into it," Darnell said. "It was before my time, so there's not much I can add, but you're welcome to have a look at it."

Paddy asked me to tell him more about the case and questioned why Aubrey and I were so interested in it.

"I've been asked that, and it's hard to answer. I'd just been at Bonfire Beach and saw a woman's body there. Then, when I read the articles about the murder that had happened there decades ago, I got caught up in the moment."

"And knowing Aubrey has such an interest in history, I'm sure she jumped right in also," Paddy said. He explained to Darnell that the old newspapers I was talking about were found here inside his pub walls.

"What a coincidence," Darnell remarked. "Good luck with all that ."

"Thanks, Chief. I just saw Jackie downstairs. You'll remember I was with her Wednesday morning. She said she handed over her videos and stills from that night. That will surely help your case."

"It will. Paddy knows the river well, so he and I were checking them out. She captured some very interesting footage of a small boat, with its running lights on, pulled up to the pier. With the timestamps on the photos, it shows it happening within the window of time of death that the doc gave us," Darnell said. "Now to find out who that might have been, and was it a planned meeting with Mrs. Turner?"

"Do you have some ideas about that?" I asked.

"A couple. Paddy already asked me about the husband, which is often where we look first in a case like this, but his alibi is solid. Chris Pratt seems very forthcoming with information, but there are times my radar signals beep when I think about him."

"I heard they met up at Shaw's that night."

"You heard right. Both the husband and Mr. Pratt commented on her drinking habits. He described her showing up at Shaw's and demanding he give her some sort of folio his mother had made up. He told her the packets would be given out when the group was at Bonfire Beach in the morning and not before. According to everyone I interviewed at Shaw's, Mrs. Turner was very aggressive toward him. So much so that he left to go out night fishing."

"And you believe Chris?" Paddy pinched his lips. "Seems he got pretty upset with her. Maybe he didn't go out fishing."

"He's on my person of interest list and so is Frances Eastwood. Eve told me what happened at the football field, which was further escalated by Ms. Eastwood's presence at Shaw's on Tuesday night, where Mrs. Turner got into her face again. My third person of interest is a man at the bar who seemed to take a particular interest in the good-looking but inebriated woman."

"You have your plate full. Lots of possibilities," I said. The woman I'd met in the Coffee Corner just a few days ago had left a trail of upset people for Darnell to question.

Darnell stood, adjusted his trousers, and put his hat

on. "Yes, ma'am. But Katie, I'm glad you came up here because you are just the person to help me out. Someone has been brought to my attention as having made threatening remarks about Mrs. Turner."

"Sure, happy to help." In an instant, the scene with Loretta on Tuesday morning flashed through my mind. Darnell must have read my thoughts.

"You know who I mean, don't you? Please tell me what that was about," Darnell said.

With a lump in my throat, I let Darnell know about Loretta and Betty Jo's relationship as I understood it. "Yes, she was upset and blew off some steam Tuesday morning. But don't we all know people who just rub us the wrong way? She left the murder scene with me on Wednesday morning, and last night at book club, she left early. It might just be that she's fighting a cold or flu. But there's nothing in her actions that point to wanting to murder her old friend."

Darnell didn't respond immediately but paused in the doorway on his way out to say, "Sometimes we've got to step back to see clearly."

CHAPTER FIFTEEN

Aubrey was waiting with me when Vincent arrived at the pub. He'd never been here but heard about it from some of his friends. I gave him a quick tour before we left for Shaw's River Lodge. He knew Aubrey's great-aunt and told a few good stories about her as we rode to Shaw's River Lodge.

When I reached out to Ken Shaw this morning and mentioned what we were interested in, he promised to dig out any records they had from the time period that Tilly worked there.

We walked into the modest lobby of the lodge. The lunch crowd had gone, but the lingering smells of fried seafood wafted from the restaurant. The space was small and cozy, with wooden walls that bore the marks of time. A few worn but comfortable chairs upholstered in a faded green-and-tan plaid were clustered around a coffee table. In one corner, a wire rack displayed local maps, brochures about fishing tours, and pamphlets for nearby attractions. Behind the scarred wooden counter hung a few shelves stocked with sunblock, bug spray, T-shirts, baseball caps, and souvenir mugs for sale.

It was evident that Jesse's handsome appearance came from his father. Ken shared the same dark hair and brown eyes, and his chiseled features softened with his smile, just like Jesse's. I was surprised to discover Darnell was here, too. He was just leaving with Jesse, and they both acknowledged us before stepping outside, right before Chris Pratt entered through a side door. Had he been waiting there to avoid talking to the police? I wouldn't blame him. What started out as a request from his mother had turned into a nightmare for him.

"Ken, can I rent that fishing boat another day? I'm still stuck here. Feel like I'm in a prison," Chris said. "Might as well be fishing to pass the day."

"Sure," Ken said. "Jesse said you caught some good ones yesterday. Hope the fishing is as good today."

"With luck, I'll bring you some to fry up for my dinner," he said as he turned to leave.

Chris didn't seem to recognize me. I'm sure he had his attention focused elsewhere on Wednesday morning, so I reintroduced myself.

"Yeah, guess I remember seeing you there."

"What a mess. Sorry you're caught up in this all, Chris," I said. "You just missed the chief."

"That was on purpose. I know I'm a suspect, all because of that woman, Betty Jo," Chris said, his upper lip curling up in disdain. "What a stupid stereotypical Southern name. She's got some nerve. Coming here demanding we all hop to for her."

"Did you give her the packet your mother had prepared?"

"I didn't. She came at me the wrong way about it. Pissed me off. I told she'd have to wait until the next morning, the same as everyone. I think my mother always suspected Betty Jo had something to do with Tilly's death but couldn't prove anything."

"Oh, really?" That was some big news. Could Linda have written it in her notes to Betty Jo? Maybe that's why she wanted to get her hands on them early, so no one else would be reading over her shoulder.

"Yeah, really. But I'm not getting caught up in the past. It's done. I just want to get out of here," Chris said.

"Her husband is in town now. Maybe you could give it to him."

"I suppose so. But my mother didn't want these to go to anyone but the person they were addressed to. Thanks a lot, Mom." Chris raised his fist upward. "Now what? Look, I'm trying to get home. Out of this wacky mess. But for now, the river is as far away as I can get."

"Maybe the packet should go to the police?"

"You know what? At this point, I could care less who gets it. Betty Jo is the name on the packet, and she is not worried about it anymore. I think I'll just throw it out."

"No, wait." I couldn't let that happen. We had to know what Linda had written to Betty Jo. It might hold a clue to solving her murder. "If you're going to throw it out, can I please have it? My friend and I are working on the case involving Tilly's death. You just spoke about your mom's suspicions. There could be something in there that might help us."

With frustration evident in his voice, and a dismissive wave of his hand, Chris said, "Forget about it. I'm done with all this. Soon as the police clear me to leave, I'm out of here. And the packet is going out with the garbage." He spun and stomped back out the side door.

Ken stepped up to me. "Was he bothering you?"

"No. It's fine."

"Our usual bartender told me he got an earful when Chris and Betty Jo talked. Then another woman, Frankie Eastwood, Tilly's sister, joined them. She lives near here and drops in quite a bit. When she saw Betty Jo sitting at the bar, the proverbial fireworks started."

Frankie had been here that night too. What did that

mean? Had she poured more fuel on the situation? "And you told this to the police?"

"We did. Chris was no dummy," Ken said. "He didn't want to get between those two and all the old baggage they had. He paid his bill and said he was going for a walk along the riverfront or night fishing. Just something to escape."

"What were they arguing about?"

"I was swamped with work, so I didn't catch all of it. But things got pretty intense, and then Frankie stormed out, too," Ken explained. "Betty Jo stayed behind, chatting and flirting with the guys at the bar. She seemed really intoxicated, so my guess is that someone offered her a ride or followed her out to make sure she didn't drive in that state."

Ken encouraged me to join Aubrey and Vincent in the restaurant. They sat at one of the dining room tables with old, oversized ledgers stacked in front of them.

"I pulled out those guest logs you asked about and found some old photo albums my father, Hank kept, too."

Ken seemed to enjoy showing us the photographs from the past. One of them was a black-and-white aerial shot showing the layout of the lodge and the cabins. Things were basically the same, though less of the grounds were groomed back then and the place appeared more rustic. Some updating was obvious, like docks and new metal roofs on the lodge and cottages since this photo was taken.

Ken enjoyed telling stories about those years of working with his father. The groups of men that would come in from out of state to spend the week here. The camaraderie of roughing it away from their everyday lives. Their businesses. Their wives. He mentioned a few political figures and big-time business leaders whose names Aubrey and I didn't recognize, but Vincent sure did.

"Those were good times. Broke some records for sizes of fish caught. Some guests made it a family affair, bringing their sons. The kids would cut loose while their dads played poker at night," Ken said. "I was only in my twenties, but Pa kept me busy working."

"And you remember Tilly?" I asked.

"Sure do," Ken said with a gleam in his eye. "She was a looker. The older men behaved respectfully to our staff. But I know she caught the eye of some of the young men who were here."

Ken was turning pages in the photo album, pointing out some of the groups that were photographed. "Pa wanted to run a fishing lodge that wealthy people would want to come back to. It would be more lucrative with free-spending clients to guide."

From what I could see, the clothing they wore looked expensive. Khaki trousers, plaid shirts, fishing vests with an abundance of pockets.

"Sharp dressers," Vincent said. "Just look at the waders and fishing gear they had. Impressive bunch."

"Here are some from the years Tilly worked here," Ken said, peering through his reading glasses. "Things aren't in the best order, but a few of these are labeled."

I sat down, taking the album from Ken. All those faces shaded by brimmed hats. Holding up a big catch or a stringer of smaller fish. Groups of men of all ages and sizes who had passed through here at one time. Had one of them murdered Tilly?

Jesse's warm breath tickled the back of my neck as he came up close behind me, his hand braced against the table for support. "What is it you're searching for, Katie?" His voice was low, sending unexpected tingles down my spine.

Don't be silly, Katie. Get a grip and calm down. I took a deep breath before I looked up at him… he was so close. With an unsteady waver in my voice I said, "Ah, I'm… I mean we're investigating a murder that happened over forty years ago. The victim was a young woman who worked here and was found dead by the old pier."

As I turned the page of the photo album, my hand

lightly brushed against his. Taking my time, I traced my finger over the handwritten names beneath some of the pictures, still trying to steady my breathing. All I could focus on were his muscular, tanned forearms below the rolled-up sleeves of his olive drab shirt.

"I've got to run now, Katie, but I'm hoping there will be a break in the action here soon, and I can take an afternoon off. Maybe take you fishing again?"

"I'd like that," I whispered.

Aubrey cleared her throat. I looked up, and she gave me a conspiratorial wink.

"At trial, the attorneys hinted that Tilly had been seeing someone besides Jimmy," Vincent said. "Did any of these young boys make advances on her?"

"I suppose it could have happened, but manners and civility were more important then. If there was trouble of any sort, the parents made the kids own up to it. Not nowadays. I've had damage done, staring us in the face. But the parents will give me the question, are you accusing my son of doing that? All the while, the kid stands there smirking. We've put up with a lot of disrespect over the years just to keep them coming back. Jesse's much better at calling them out on it than I ever was."

"That's how you raised me, Dad," Jesse said. "I remember Grandpa could be pretty tough on you."

Aubrey had been photographing pages of the guest and visitor logs. Without looking up, she said, "I'm sure they ogled her. Some of those guys you talked about must have been close to her age. Think about it. To a small-town girl, they were intriguing. Handsome, big city boys with money to throw around."

"You make a good point," Ken said. "Back then it seemed girls like Tilly were sort of expected to stay in Seaside Cove and raise a family. But I think she had an itch to get out. As the attraction of the big shot high school quarterback faded, she saw Jimmy as someone who would never leave," Ken said. "He started getting grease under his fingernails and needing a shave. Marge and I were dating then, and she's the one who pointed that out to me after Tilly died."

Aubrey had a good idea. I decided to take cell phone shots of the photos, too. Thank goodness for technology. We could review them later once we'd gathered more information. These photographs might take on new meaning. Or was this a silly goose chase?

On our way back to town, Aubrey, Vincent, and I made a stop at the pier. Vincent insisted on seeing it again, explaining that being in the actual locations mentioned in his reporting helped him to better understand and remember the events. He spoke about the pier's significance for local teenagers. He walked along the sandy beach, looking north, in the direction of Shaw's River Lodge, trying to recall if there was ever a walking path between here and the lodge. He mentioned that the police thought it was likely how Tilly got here on the night of her murder.

It was intriguing observing him. Here was someone who had totally immersed himself in the very thing we were attempting to revive.

What would be the end result this time?

CHAPTER SIXTEEN

The call from Blaire letting us know we could see the case file from the Eastwood murder came just as I was turning onto Main Street. It was a no-brainer that all of us wanted to go immediately to check it out.

Blaire escorted us to one of the side rooms at the police station. "There's not much here as far as physical evidence, but you might be interested in some of the paperwork. I'll be up in the front if you need anything. I can make copies for you, but according to the rules, nothing leaves this room."

"Sorry, Blaire, but we came directly from Shaw's and didn't bring pen and paper," I said.

"I've got you covered on that." She returned quickly with paper, pens, Post-it notes, and bottled water. "Some of these case files can be pretty tough to look at, so take your time."

First, we checked out the crime scene photographs. Vincent studied them calmly and methodically while Aubrey's breaths came out heavy and uneven, clearly uncomfortable with the images of young Matilda Eastwood. As for me, I struggled to keep my breakfast down as my stomach threatened to rebel against the gruesome images.

Vincent quickly noted that there appeared to be a path along the river, both coming into Bonfire Beach and then continuing on the shoreline toward Seaside Cove. "It was clearly used, but this afternoon looked pretty grown over. So this shows that Tilly could have easily walked there after she got off work. There was an almost full moon and a clear night, so it won't have been hard to stay on the path."

"And so could the killer," Aubrey said. "He could have come from either direction and left either way, too."

Vincent was most familiar with what police reports and witness interviews read like, so he pulled those aside and began to read them while Aubrey turned her attention to any bagged evidence in the box.

I reached for a small book at the bottom of the box. It was a diary. This had to have belonged to Tilly! The pink cover was decorated with whimsical butterflies and hearts, and there was a small metal clasp with a keyhole for a tiny key that had once protected her private thoughts. As I opened to the first page, there it was, *Property of...Matilda Eastwood.* Holding this physical piece of her past in my hands, I felt a strong connection to Tilly, as if she were communicating with me from beyond the grave. I shuddered at the thought of the police handling this diary. Her dreams, hopes, and everyday musings were all exposed on these pages. The pages inside were lined in pale blue, and her neat handwriting filled every inch of space with words and doodles.

I began to skim through her writings but then realized I had to meet Eve in an hour. I'd better hurry. Tilly referenced people by initials. *J* showed up on many of the pages, it had to be Jimmy, and I assumed the *L* I saw stood for Linda. It was hard to skip over so many pages, but I fought the temptation to read each page. I had to focus on the time period prior to her murder.

Finally got up the nerve to go for a tarot card reading, F took me to see the lady in the woods. E was nice and worked with me to let my thoughts guide both of us.

That had to be *E* for Ella. Tilly recorded the tarot card reading Ella remembered. Frankie, her sister, must be the *F* she wrote about because, within a few pages, she wrote more.

F asked me and after getting her word that she won't tell the folks, I confessed I was preggers. It's hard to even put that in writing.

Throughout the summer more and more entries mentioned B, suggesting she was growing apart from Jimmy. She expressed confusion and guilt and how bad she felt about what was going on. There was a muddled and confused tone to her entries. She began to write of her dream of marrying B. So, he must have been the father. Poor Jimmy was being two-timed. Who was this mysterious B who was getting more and more hearts drawn around his name? At the end of summer, her old friends returned to college, and she wrote about how distant she felt from them now. A desperate feeling came through in her entries after that.

B has gone back to his home and left me his wrong phone number. What can I do? I should have told him about it sooner.

The watery smudges must have come from her tears. Whoever *B* was, he didn't live here, and she didn't even have the guy's correct number. Had he tricked her by giving her a wrong number, or had it been an innocent mistake? But a day later, she found a way to contact him.

I'm so relieved that I found his uncle's info in the register and called him. Left a message.

A doodle of praying hands was next to this entry.

I'd become so caught up in Tilly's life that Blaire's entry to our room startled me. "How are you all doing in here? Did you come up with anything for me to copy?"

"I did," Vincent said. "I can make them if you just point me to the copy machine."

"Blaire, is there a way to check out Tilly's diary from the evidence box? I'd really like to read more, but I have a commitment and can't stay any longer. In fact, I'm meeting with your grandmother, Eve."

"Let me check with Darnell. In a case this old, I can't see it would really matter," Blaire said.

"I was wondering what you were so absorbed in," Aubrey said. "You were like in another world. There isn't much physical evidence in here. They found a note in Tilly's pocket, but the water had messed with the ink, and I couldn't read it. But I got really interested in reading the police report and witness statements with Vincent."

"I'm glad he's copying those," I said. "Gosh, I wish I didn't have to run. We've got to get together later and go over the things we've discovered. Could you bring the diary if Darnell gives the okay?"

"Sure. Why are you going to Eve's?" Aubrey asked.

"Do you remember I told you that their friend made up letters, little packets for each of the Secret Sisters? Well, we got to talking about it at book club and I thought maybe Linda, the historian of the group, had some information about Tilly in here. Sort of a random hope, I know, but Eve said she'd show me hers today."

Vincent returned to the room with his copies of the reports and interviews. He announced he was leaving now, too, and would review everything he copied later.

Aubrey seemed surprised we both were leaving, but she said she'd wait here for the diary and walk home afterward.

"Jimmy hasn't returned my call," Vincent said as he put the original paperwork back in the case file box, "but I'll reach out to him again right when I get home. Hopefully, he'll agree to meet us. You guys would be up for that, right?"

"Absolutely. With what I just read in her diary, we need to talk directly with Jimmy and get his side of things. Let's touch base later this afternoon."

CHAPTER SEVENTEEN

The Polaroid photograph Eve handed to me was faded. The colors softened and blurred with age. In it, a group of young people smiled at the camera, their faces full of innocence and promise. But my eyes were drawn to one girl in particular, her hair cascading in soft waves over her shoulders, her eyes sparkling with mischief. It was Matilda Eastwood, the girl who had drowned at Bonfire Beach so many years ago.

"That was in my packet from Linda," Eve said. "Along with my People magazine interview and other promotional things printed about me over the years."

"Mine contained clippings from the Cove Gazette," Loretta said. "And a short note about us losing touch with each other. Linda always was the bond that held our group together in high school and after."

I'd been surprised to see Loretta here with Eve, but when she explained that Darnell had called her in after someone overheard her saying she wanted to strangle Betty Jo's neck, I understood her needing some friendly support.

"Who had been nearby us that morning? Was someone in the hall or maybe coming out of the Coffee Corner?" I asked.

Loretta didn't look me in the eye as she replied, "I was too focused on my anger with Betty Jo to notice. But now, answer me honestly. I'll understand if it was you, Katie."

"No! Absolutely not. I knew it was just hyperbole. Who would have even thought anything else or even know who we were talking about?"

"Don't you remember? I said her entire name for emphasis. Stupid. Stupid me."

I felt so bad for Loretta. I knew how much Betty Jo got under her skin. "I'm sure Darnell doesn't suspect you of murder, though. What else did he ask you?"

"He asked when the last time I saw or spoke to her was, and I told him about how she called me Tuesday night, wanting to meet up. I told her no because it would have been pointless. But now I can't help feeling guilty. Maybe she wouldn't have died if I'd met her somewhere." Loretta's head dropped into her hands.

Eve reached out to comfort her with a gentle touch on her shoulder. "You couldn't have known Loretta. That's water under the bridge. Things that we can't go back and change, no matter how much we wish it to be so."

Loretta sighed. "Had I at least joined you and Peaches for dinner, I would have an alibi for part of the evening."

"Stop it! You don't need an alibi. Darnell is working hard on the case and will find the killer." I looked down at the photograph in my hand. A young life ended too soon. She deserved to have her case solved, too. "Aubrey, Vincent, and I were there to look at old registrations to dig deeper into Tilly's murder."

"Katie, I'm sure Linda would be so grateful to know about that. We'll help you any way we can," Loretta said.

Eve handed me a handwritten letter. "You came because you wanted to see my letter from Linda. Well, here it is."

I took a few minutes to read the note...

Dearest Eve...I still had your parents' address so I hope you got the letters I wrote over the years. I read your book about high school buddies and friendships. Where the Road Ends was fascinating. I kept trying to see if any of us were written into it. I think Loretta may have been the Sharon character, or am I imagining that? Corrine had to be

Peaches with her lighthearted humor and positive outlook. But I was flummoxed reading about a murder with what could only be described as parallels to our sister Tilly's death. Did you know more than you shared with us or the police at the time? Neither here nor there now, but I've always wished for resolution with that. What is it they call it now, closure? If you're reading this, it means I'm gone and we didn't reconnect to solve Tilly's murder. Maybe each of us has a piece of knowledge and if you put them all together her murderer could be brought to justice. Forever xoxoxo Linda

Did Eve use a tragedy in her own life as fodder for a story? Did the Secret Sisters know more about Tilly's murder than they shared? Eve was not reacting to my throat clearing sounds. I had to press her here. "So did you know something or suspect something you could have shared back then?" I asked, handing the letter back to her.

Eve leaned back and looked pensively out toward the lights on Horseshoe Island. "As authors, our ideas can come from a multitude of sources. Is it possible that one of my buried memories resurfaced while writing? I suppose it's possible, but I've been wracking my brain since I received Linda's note and heard you were investigating the cold case. Unfortunately, nothing stands out that could assist you. I do draw inspiration from people

I know when crafting characters, but no single character is based entirely on someone in my life."

"I appreciate you putting some more thought into it. Aubrey and I are making some progress. We got to look at the police files from that case. Vincent Pahlke, the reporter who covered the case, is trying to convince Jimmy to talk with us."

"You know, that reminds me of a scene at our dorm after we heard Tilly had been murdered. I found Betty Jo's reaction to it very disturbing. I attributed it to jealousy. She was trying to act upset, but it all seemed fake. It felt insincere."

"Why would she be jealous of Tilly to that extent?" I asked.

"Betty Jo Kunkel was more of a classic beauty," Eve said. "You saw her. She aged well. Tilly was what the young guys called hot. When we were in high school, Betty Jo tried to steal Jimmy away, but it didn't work. It became a source of embarrassment for her when everyone found out."

Loretta nodded. "I remember that time. She always made everything about her, even back then. And it only got worse as time went by. Actually, there is something I've been meaning to bring up. It may be what Betty Jo wanted to discuss with me."

She proceeded to tell us about a chance encounter in

Atlanta that cemented her feelings about Betty Jo. "I was at a family wedding with my husband Arnie. We ran into Betty Jo and Neil in the lobby, who were attending some fancy law gala. Betty Jo bragged about Neil's prestigious firm, their multi-million-dollar home in Buckhead, her tennis pro, and so on and so on. Then we went our separate ways.

"Later on, as Arnie and I were trying to find our way from the ballroom wing to our hotel room, we turned a corner and saw Neil with another woman. With one hand braced against the wall, he pressed his body against hers. His other hand wandered to places it had no business being. Luckily, they didn't seem to notice us watching.

"I debated telling Betty Jo about what I saw but ultimately decided that if it were me, I would want to know. When I finally mustered up the courage to tell her, she exploded in anger and accused me of lying and being envious of her seemingly perfect life. Her words stung like a slap in the face."

"Wow," Eve exclaimed. "That was quite a random thing. Did she ever come back to you after the initial shock and explain anything? Because I can see why she adamantly denied that her husband might be cheating. That's a hard thing to face."

"Oh, she got back to me alright. Telling me how

lucky I am that she's the sort to rise above such betrayal from a friend but that I had stuck my nose in where it wasn't welcome and that I was never again to bring this up. She said she would accept my apology, which I didn't give. Then she slammed the phone down."

"How long ago was this?"

"Arnie's been gone over ten years, so I'd say maybe nineteen, twenty years ago," Loretta said. "Could this be a case of once a cheater always a cheater, or was it a one-and-done?"

I realized what Loretta told us didn't help with the cold case, but it might be something Darnell could use. "Don't you think you should tell Darnell about this?"

Exasperation and exhaustion washed over Loretta, causing her shoulders to droop in weariness. This situation was draining all of her energy. "Honestly, I don't see the point. It happened so long ago. And I can't even explain why I'm sharing it here in this moment except that it might help you both recognize that my disdain for, God rest her soul, Betty Jo, comes from a deeper place than everyone thinks."

Eve stood and went to hug Loretta. "It's okay, honey. I'm glad you got it off your chest."

What a story. Perhaps both she and Neil had affairs over the years and that led to Betty Jo's flirtatious behavior at Shaw's Tuesday night. I didn't want to get tangled up in this current situation. I had enough to do investigating the cold case. A text came in from Vincent, saying he would be at the pub with Jimmy for happy hour. Good news. I'd hear his side of the story directly from his mouth.

Not second-hand.

Not from a news article.

CHAPTER EIGHTEEN

It was nice to see Jack and Scott in the pub when I got there. Neil Turner was with them, so I was able to meet him and personally extend my sympathy. Neil was a thin man and rather ordinary-looking, but he exuded confidence and politely accepted my condolences. The image Loretta left in my mind just hours earlier didn't fit with the man in front of me now. Maybe it had been a one-off transgression on his part, or Betty Jo stuck with her disbelief, and they worked through it. Either way, this was a man who'd just lost his wife in a horrendous way.

"I'm grateful that my buddy Jack got me out fishing today. It really helped get me through another day without Betty Jo," Neil said after I asked how the fishing went.

"He's quite the fisherman," Jack said. "It's a side of him I never knew."

"That's good to hear. Did you meet Betty Jo here in Seaside Cove?" I asked.

"No. We got together at college." He tapped his finger on the Emory logo on his polo shirt. "She transferred to the school, and we have been together ever since then."

Liam asked us if we wanted another drink. I declined, but the men ordered.

"Neil, how long will you be here? I'm sure Eve and Peaches and Loretta would like to meet you."

"Ah, the Secret Sisters," Neil said as a soft smile tugged at his lips. "Betty Jo loved them all so much and had been looking forward to this visit. I'm meeting them here for brunch tomorrow before I leave town."

"Oh, good. Scott, did Jackie and Sophia have a good time at the beach today?"

"Yes, they did. Too good of a time with Tyler," Jack said. "Guess he makes a killer umbrella drink. The outcome being that they are staying in tonight. I don't know what happened there, but they mumbled something about what happens at the Rum Runner stays at the Rum Runner."

Tyler was always such a stand-up guy. He made sure my friends and I were well taken care of, and I couldn't help but chuckle at the sight of them enjoying their drinks at the Rum Runner. For me, one of those umbrella drinks is about all I can do without getting loopy. Hanging out with friends on the beach doesn't sound bad, but not until after this cold case was worked out. It felt like we were really making progress.

Aubrey arrived and greeted Liam with a quick hug, then led me to a secluded table where Vincent sat with Jimmy Conrad and an amiable-looking, gray-haired woman. From the early photos of him, I would never have guessed that the portly man with a round, chubby face had once been a state-champion high school quarterback. However, when he smiled, I caught a glimpse of what he used to be.

The couple stood and shook our hands as Vincent introduced us.

"I will warn you that I'm not really eager to talk about this, but my wife Bernice here is the one who encouraged me to come and sit a spell with y'all," Jimmy said.

I noticed they reached for each other's hands and Bernice smiled up at him as he continued. "She's always reading about other cold cases that have been solved."

"Vincent convinced me that this would be a good thing for my Jimmy," Bernice said eagerly. "He told me that you two are a couple of smart ones and he's holding out hope that you might be just the folks to finally figure out who killed Tilly. I'll help in any way I can." She eagerly leaned in toward us to inform us. "I watch a lot of cold case murder mysteries."

"Why, thanks, Bernice. Getting your husband to agree to meet us is a great start," Aubrey said.

Vincent smiled at the couple. "As we were just saying, it's been a very long time since we've talked at any length about this."

Jimmy nodded, drumming his fingers nervously on the table. "Don't know if stirring this all up again will do anyone any good."

"I have a strong feeling this will be different," I replied.

A waitress interrupted us to take orders for drinks. I requested a plate of appetizers, thinking it might help relax everyone if they had something to nibble on while we talked.

We spent a few minutes making small talk about the weather and how nice the pub looked until our waitress returned, bringing Jimmy and Bernice their coffees, Vincent his bourbon, and Aubrey and I our beers.

"Aubrey and I really appreciate you coming over," I said. "I can imagine the recent death at the pier brought up some bad memories for you. It was part of what got us engaged in solving the Eastwood murder, especially when Aubrey came across old newspapers from that time reporting on the crime."

"And luckily, we found the reporter who wrote them!" Aubrey said as she reached for a pretzel bite and dipped it in the cheese sauce.

Vincent smirked as he pointed to the cheese dripping down the side of Aubrey's mouth. "And found him still alive. Don't forget that part."

Jimmy reached for the small bowl of creamers and poured one into each of their coffees. "Vincent promised me that you weren't like the reporters and writers who showed up years later, attempting to exploit my difficult past for a sensational story. Much as my sweet wife would have liked it, none of them ever turned it into a popular TV show or documentary, trying to solve it as a cold case file."

"That's not us," Aubrey said. "No, sir. But there have been advances in the way crimes are solved, and maybe someone's memory will be jogged with this new murder."

"Okay, what do you want to ask me? I imagine Vincent has told you about how it all went down. The trial and all," Jimmy said.

Vincent rested his arms on the table and cupped the glass of golden liquid in front of him. "There's one thing

I'd like you to tell the gals about. The figure you saw walking on the road that night as you drove out to meet Tilly. I was reviewing the police report, and it was barely mentioned in there."

"They didn't seem to think it had anything to do with it. And what does it matter now? I didn't see his face cause he looked down and put his hand up to shield his eyes from my headlights. He was just some guy walking along River Road. That's about all I can say."

"I don't remember reading that in the articles. Did the police ever look for him?" I asked.

"Sure, but I think they thought I was making it up…"

Bernice spoke up with the confidence of someone who had spent hours in front of a television screen, "They're trying to pin the blame on someone else."

"They just all wanted it done with so our community could feel they were safe again. That they didn't have to fear some crazed random killer of young women was among them," Jimmy added.

"Could the person you saw have been a woman?" I asked.

"At that time of night alone on a dark road? It never crossed my mind, but I guess it could have been. The figure was slight, average height, shoulder length hair… wearing jeans and a blue jacket."

"Where was his car?"

"I didn't even notice another car on the road. All I could think about was getting to Tilly. I was early, eagerly hoping that tonight would be the night she finally said yes to my proposal." Jimmy took a deep breath and with a wistful sadness in his eyes, continued, "But after everything that came out during the trial, I realize now that I was incredibly naïve."

"Honey, you were in love." Bernice put her coffee cup down and kissed him lightly on his scruffy cheek.

"Could you have been the baby's father?" Aubrey blurted out before clapping her hand over her mouth. "Sorry, Mrs. Conrad. That was kind of rude."

"Oh dear, I know the whole story, and let's just say it would have been unlikely but not impossible."

Jimmy nodded. "You've got to remember I wanted to be with her. To work hard to make a life together here in Seaside Cove. I was in a carpenter apprenticeship program and getting ready to join the union."

I noticed Neil, Scott, and Jack exiting the pub and gave them a wave goodbye. "That's the husband of Betty Jo. He's been in town but is leaving tomorrow."

"Poor guy," Jimmy said. "We both lost someone at Bonfire Beach."

"And they were both Secret Sisters," Vincent remarked.

"Yep, they were. Now back to your questions. The

police knew about the figure on the highway but could never find him. I was the only guy they ever really suspected. The jilted boyfriend, two-timed like Tilly's diary showed. I think they saw me as the big dumb oaf. I'd gotten into an altercation in the park one night, and they tagged me as a man with a temper."

Aubrey reached into the large leather tote at her feet. "Speaking of the diary, the police department agreed to sign it out to me from the case file."

An audible gasp escaped Jimmy's mouth.

"Have you ever seen it?" she asked.

"I have. My public defender had a copy because it was brought in as evidence at the time." He glanced at the pink butterfly-covered diary before looking up at Aubrey. "I don't think I could bear looking at it now."

His wife reached for it. "May I?" She pulled the diary out and began paging through.

"Did you ever think of someone who fit the *B* character in the diary?" I asked.

Jimmy rubbed his forehead as he slowly shook his head. "Don't you think I tried? And I watched for that vivid blue color of the person's jacket all over town. But with all the Bills, Bobs, and Brians none of them fit with the quick glance I caught of the person. And like I said, back then, I wasn't thinking of Beckys, Bettys, or Bonnies."

"And if I remember correctly, you said Tilly's family had no idea either," Vincent said.

"Her parents were, how should I put it, sort of hands-off. They never even came to the football games when I was the quarterback, and she was a cheerleader. No real support from them as she was growing up. Her older sister Frankie was okay. At least she seemed to care more about finding the real murderer. To this day, I believe her parents always thought it was me."

"Frances ran into the group on your old high school football field when they were spreading ashes," I said.

"You're kidding. What was she doing there?" Jimmy asked.

"She works there in some capacity," I said. "She and Betty Jo got into a heated conversation."

"Funny, but I just had a flashback of Betty Jo putting the moves on me more than once after football games," Jimmy said with a chuckle. "She was known for that and for being self-centered. Frankie never had patience with someone like that."

"Well, as I always said, you were a hottie," Bernice added.

"In the past tense?" Jimmy's youthful smile and twinkle in his eyes showed up again. "You know what I'm thinking. You should talk to Frankie about this, too. She was almost like a mother to Tilly."

"Good idea," Vincent said. "I'll reach out to her."

Bernice closed the diary and returned it to Aubrey. "How about Jimmy tries to reach her right now? She's the only other person I can think of that might know who this *B* was."

CHAPTER NINETEEN

"Come on, we can go to our office upstairs," I said after Jimmy texted Frankie and she agreed to have a phone conversation. "You can put it on speakerphone so we can all talk together."

When Jimmy set his cell phone on my desk and put it on speaker, the first thing Frankie said was, "Let me get it straight about who all is on this call before I open my big mouth."

"Frankie, hi, it's Bernice, Jimmy's wife."

"And you must remember me, Vincent Pahlke, the reporter that interviewed you and the family."

"The other two young women here are the ones who got me caught up in your sister's case again," Jimmy said. "Katie Murphy is part owner of Paddy's Pub here in town, and Aubrey Miller is a bookkeeper. She's the one who found the old newspapers with the articles from the time of Tilly's death."

"So why are those two so interested in this?" Frankie asked in an accusatory tone. "Think there's a story for the tabloids?"

"Frankie, it's Katie," I said, leaning in to get closer to Jimmy's cell phone. "Nothing like that. I know some of the Secret Sisters, the group your sister was a part of. And I was at the pier the morning Betty Jo's body was found. When Aubrey showed me the old papers, and I learned more about your sister's case, we decided to see if we might be able to discover new information to solve it."

"So that's it? You heard about my meeting them at the football field, I suppose. Was it you who reported it to the police?"

"No!"

"Well, someone did, and I got called up on the carpet about Betty Jo's murder. Stuff gets stirred up and then gets messed up. I got a bad feeling about this whole cold case thing. Not for me. Goodnight, y'all."

Jimmy, who had been hunched over his phone with his arms propped up on my desk, dropped back into his chair in surprise, and Vincent's face contorted with disbelief. Panic flooded through me. I couldn't let her hang up on me. "I'm so sorry to hear that. But all of us here feel strongly about it. We've been gathering evidence and would like to hear your story from that awful time."

"To what end? You think playing pretend investigators will turn up anything new? The police back then claimed they found no other suspect and tried pinning it on you, Jimmy. I'm surprised you're even talking now. What's wrong with you? Didn't you suffer enough?"

Bernice's face hardened. "Frankie, it's Bernice again. I would think you'd care, too. The people sitting here with me and my husband think there are new possibilities. That new clues might be found. Cold cases are solved all the time. Plus, you must remember Linda, Tilly's roommate, who was so supportive of Jimmy through it all. She just died now too. You could at least give Katie and Aubrey a chance to explain themselves."

You go, girl, I thought. There was a moment of silence on the line. I glanced up at the expectant faces illuminated by the glow of the phone screen. Were we wrong to call Tilly's sister? Her skepticism was understandable.

Then her voice broke the silence. "I do. She was one of the good ones and was as hurt by this as my family was. But what does Linda have to do with anything?"

Aubrey turned to me and motioned for me to talk, whispering, "Tell her about the letters Linda wrote."

"Linda wrote letters to the remaining Secret Sisters to be opened after her death. She requested them to basically reopen the case and for all of them to try to help solve the murder," I blurted out. "I'm doing it for them too."

"Linda requested the third location to spread her ashes be Bonfire Beach. And I don't think it was because of the fun times they all had there," Aubrey said. "I think it was a sign of her love for Tilly and the angst of losing her way too soon."

"I heard about that," Frankie said. "Her son got in touch with me. She sent a message from before she died, that he met me and that I try to figure out the murder. So, I understand where y'all are coming from."

Whew, so Linda was really calling out the troops to find her friend's murderer. Just a few days ago, we were singing Auld Lang Syne as the new year started off with a bang, and now this group was brought together by a woman who never forgot old friends.

"So, will you help?" Jimmy asked.

There was no response.

"Are you still there?" Vincent said.

"She better not have hung up on us," Aubrey said. "It's her very own sister's murderer we're trying to find, for Pete's sake. Well, if that's her thank you to Linda, we'll do this without her."

"Oh, cool your jets." We all sighed with relief when we heard Frankie's voice again. "If I'm gonna sit here and talk about that time, I figured I'd get a beer and move to the porch. I'm gonna need to be looking up at the stars, hoping Tilly's giving me some strength. If you all are ready, take a seat and listen up 'cause I ain't repeating myself."

The five of us in the office at Paddy's Pub settled in to listen to Frances's memories of that time. She knew that the death consumed Linda for years after the murder. Occasionally she'd spoken to Linda after she moved away, but their conversations had ended about three years ago.

According to Frankie, her sister was a typical small-town girl. She loved being a cheerleader and always made sure she dressed nicely, even if that meant she wore the same outfit more than once a week. She suspected Tilly was pregnant even before she confirmed it because she noticed her breasts were getting bigger.

This was early fall, so it wouldn't be surprising if one of the visiting fishermen or entitled kids could have gotten her knocked up. But Frankie explained that she kept that thought to herself and just asked her sister if Jimmy was going to step up and marry her.

I cringed at the blunt words, but I now knew Frankie had a no-nonsense way of speaking, and I'd heard worse. Glancing across the desk to Jimmy, he seemed close to tears. Vincent was completely focused on what was being said.

She continued, telling us that this was when she first learned that her sister had been sleeping with another man and that when Tilly confronted him, he demanded she get an abortion.

"Hang on, Frankie," Aubrey said. "You brought up the fishermen who stayed at the lodge. Do you think this *B* character could have been one of them?"

"Sure. Tilly never told me much about the guy. Lord forgive me, but I was so angry with her for getting into this situation that she stopped talking to me about it."

Jimmy looked faint, so I texted Liam downstairs to have a waitress bring us some waters. I didn't want to miss a word of what was being said here.

"I told the police about all of this, and so did Linda," Frankie said. "Both of us thought that it could have been a tourist that turned Tilly's head. And we both had a strong feeling some money or influence had exchanged hands because the police didn't seem to care much about looking for the guy. They were focused only on Jimmy. I knew how that worked. We were white trash to them rich folk from out of state."

"But I seem to remember they investigated the people at the lodge," Vincent said. "But they couldn't find anyone who saw Tilly together with a specific man. And she certainly never reported a rape."

A loud snort came over the phone. "Course they didn't 'cause they didn't try very hard. It would mess with the lucrative tourist trade."

"Did you learn anything when you went to see Linda's son Chris at Shaw's Tuesday night?" Aubrey asked.

"Hard to say. He seemed edgy. Nervous."

"Maybe he was just weary of all the drama?" Aubrey said. "You seemed tuned into people, Frankie. Think about it. Maybe there was something from that night that could be connected to the past case."

"He said he was getting some fishing in while he was here on the river. Then, as we sipped our beers, he asked me to retell the story of Tilly because he'd only heard his mother's side of it. My tongue loosened a bit, and I told him I suspected Tilly wasn't the only gal in Seaside Cove that these out-of-town fellas snuggled up to. He tells me his mom, Linda, said the same thing and had warned Tilly not to mess around with them and not to cheat on Jimmy because there were lots of girls who would gladly take him off Tilly's hands..."

At those words, Bernice whispered to Jimmy, "I had my eyes on you for years, honey. I was patient."

"Including that Betty Jo. But then she had a reputation for stealing boyfriends. She's a piece of work. Rich b...sorry, my sailor's mouth can get me in trouble. But she went and got belligerent with Chris over some stupid papers and then started getting aggressive with me for lord knows what. She ended up saying her husband's a lawyer, and she'll sue us and blah, blah, blah. I don't know where all that came from except to say she was totally wasted. What a joke. I do remember one of the guys at the bar, who was hitting on her, offered to give her a ride home if she needed one."

"Chris told us the same story this morning. He said he left the lodge. So do you know what happened after he took off?" I asked.

"She got a phone call she didn't like. As soon as she hung up, her messy lipstick-stained mouth tightened into a thin line. Then she came back and threw her arm around the guy and told him she'd take him up on that offer. Here's this sixty-something broad trying to be all sexy and cute. It was pathetic." Frankie spit out the last words and then let out a loud, harsh laugh. "But the guy says forget it, lady. Must have seen her in a better light and realized what she really looked like. Listen, that's all I know. I've got to let the dog out to do his business. Hope you guys figure this out."

CHAPTER TWENTY

When Frankie hung up, Bernice decided it was time for her and Jimmy to leave. Vincent followed shortly after them, saying it was getting close to his bedtime and that we could talk more tomorrow. Aubrey stood and started gathering up the glasses of water.

"No, you don't," I said. "Those glasses can wait. I'm more interested in finding out what all those Post-it notes are for in Tilly's diary pages."

"I love sticky notes! I snagged these from Blaire when we were at the police station. There's a lot in here," Aubrey said. "Sure you don't want to wait until morning?"

"I'm sure! I've been thinking about all we gathered up today between Shaw's and the cold case file examination. I want to get it a little better organized in my brain before I go to sleep tonight. Things are criss-crossing in my head. Cold case. Current case. It seems that anytime I try to focus in on the cold case, information about the current murder investigation sticks its nose in."

Aubrey reached for the diary. "I get what you mean. But don't be too hard on yourself, my friend. Remember, you're dealing with the new case more than me or Vincent. Dare I say that makes me more clearheaded? He's gone home to bed, so I guess it's up to me to fill you in."

She was right. I'd been involved with the new murder since Tuesday morning when I met Betty Jo, and Loretta told me she could strangle her. Then, being there at the scene on Wednesday morning pulled me in even more. And it didn't stop there because when I met with the book club Thursday night, it was on everyone's mind. Again, I witnessed how they, especially Loretta, were affected by Betty Jo's murder. And now, today, it seemed our attempt to focus our efforts on Tilly was thwarted by what we learned had happened at the lodge Tuesday night.

"Knock knock. Anyone home, Katie?"

I gave my head a sharp shake. "Sorry Aubrey. My brain is on overload, and I short-circuited there for a moment."

Aubrey cocked her head and touched my forehead as though feeling for a fever. "You've caught the cold case bug, haven't you?"

I shifted in my seat and took a long sip of my water. "Okay, tell me about what you found."

"This is the first time that the initial *B* appeared. The entry was made early in the summer. I'm trying not to read between the lines, but boy oh boy, she picked out *B* pretty quick and acted on her attraction." Aubrey handed me the diary, her finger on the point where I should start reading...

Super busy at work tonight. A big group from Montgomery left yesterday and tips were really good. Now another gang from Atlanta took over five of the cabins. The usual older guys, but some are around my age which is fun. Two of them, B and T, are trying to get me to show them around Seaside. Haha maybe I will. They are cute.

"This goes on for a while, and she begins to only write about the *B* guy. Then we read some of this at the lodge earlier today. She's getting more involved with him. Obviously, because we know how close they got," Aubrey said with a nudge into my ribs. "There's a period where he's gone back home. Tilly told us about him wanting her to get an abortion. Here is the entry about that night I want you to read."

B called me again while I was at work. I had to talk to

him! Even though they don't like us taking personal calls. Apologized for being such a jerk and said he has to drive down and hold me. See me. Apologize and make things right.

A big heart encircled the next few words.

I think he wants to ask me to marry him and make this right. I want to talk to L. B told me not to talk to anyone. His father is being awful about it. College and all that. I don't know what to do.

"We heard Jimmy say he got there early that night," I said.

"He did. That girl was sure getting things tangled up, wasn't she?"

"Maybe *B* arrived unexpectedly early, too? So, he was the figure Jimmy saw on the road. The exact timing of their plans is a mystery. And since the man was driving, it's unlikely that their meetup was scheduled down to the minute," I suggested.

"But why would he be walking on the road? Wouldn't he just park by the beach?"

"That's pretty obvious, Aubrey. He didn't want his car to be seen because he had nefarious plans," I said.

"Duh." Aubrey smacked her forehead with her hand. "You're right. Anyway, I flagged these comments to send to Vincent. He checked his data from the registries. And let me tell you, old man Vincent is pretty darn good with computers. He used an app that scanned the registers and created PDFs, then emailed me the groups he narrowed it down to, but none of their names start with a B."

Now that's impressive, I thought as I looked at Vincent's email. So the man we're looking for was in his early twenties and going to college likely within a few hundred miles radius. Aubrey began searching for more elite colleges, narrowing them down to ones with blue in their school colors.

Meanwhile, I called Ken Shaw to see if he remembered any of the parties that summer where kids wore college jackets or gear. He said there were lots of them. When I told him about the parameters of color, he suggested Emory. "And Katie," Ken said. "I came across questionable financial issues in the old accounting books. Things that don't jibe with what I remember. I'll keep notes on it and when we can get together, I'd be happy to share it with you and Aubrey."

"Listen," I said to Aubrey. "I'm going to get us a coffee downstairs while you check out the Emory yearbooks for our guy."

She slumped back in her chair. "Are you serious? We don't even know what he looks like. Now what? We pull up the online yearbook and look for, oh, let's see, all the

Roberts, Williams, Benjamins, and Blakes? Why oh why didn't she just use their name? It would make this so much easier."

"Aubrey. Not that way! Use the last names in what Vincent sent over. There aren't that many different ones. It's a start, at least. I'll be right back."

CHAPTER TWENTY-ONE

Darnell and Paddy sat comfortably at the curve of the wooden bar, enjoying a cold pint after a day of work. Paddy had retired as the chief of police in Harmony, Wisconsin, and their shared interest in law enforcement brought them together as friends. Plus, Darnell often sought Paddy's advice and perspective on different cases he was working on.

"Hey, Katie," Paddy said. "Is your meeting over?"

"No way. We're just hitting our stride," I answered.

"Is there anything I can do to help you?" Darnell asked.

I raised my eyebrow and elongated my response. "Well...how much time do you have? Would you be willing to go upstairs, and I'll show you where we're at?"

Aubrey was surprised to see Paddy and Darnell enter

the office behind me and grab a seat. "Big chiefs to the rescue? We welcome your arrival!"

Darnell chuckled. "Don't know about that, but I'd like to hear what you have so far."

"After you left the lodge yesterday, we went through photo albums and registration ledgers," Aubrey said. "We also spoke to Jimmy Conrad and Frances, Tilly's sister. With all the information we've gathered, we're at the point of possibly identifying the mysterious man mentioned in Tilly's diary. By the way, thanks for letting me check that evidence out."

"My pleasure," Darnell said.

"Without going into all the details right now, I'll summarize our conclusion," I said. "We've surmised the guy was probably here with family, staying in cabins at Shaw's where he met Tilly. He was the father of her baby. We believe he went to Emory University and came back here in the fall and murdered her."

"Whoa, ladies! That's a pretty big leap, isn't it?" Paddy said. "Katie, you've told me a bit about the case, but I understood the police at the time didn't have a suspect except the boyfriend. And he was exonerated at trial. Are you saying that forty years later, you found all this out in a matter of days?"

"It sounds extraordinary when you put it that way, but the simple answer is yes."

Aubrey was back at her computer screen and had photographs from the albums at Shaw's pulled up. "Most of these had minimal identifying information on them, but I isolated three photographs that might contain a photo of the mysterious *B*. I found a dozen possible Emory students through the last name. It's only a start, but I thought this might give me something to compare them to."

Looking at the screen over her shoulder, I said, "I have a program I use here for graphics for our publicity. It should be able to sharpen and enlarge these and the online college yearbook photos you've found. Then we might be able to use a Google image search to help, too, in case we need it."

"I'm impressed, but girls, you realize this might be impossible to prove," Darnell said. "It's been so long."

"But the story makes sense. He would have had means and motive," Aubrey said.

"But stop and think. Why, when all this was fresh in the minds of Seaside Cove, didn't anyone at Shaw's help identify and find this young man?" Paddy said. "It seems like a reach that the police at that time wouldn't have at least brought him up as a suspect."

"That's where the story takes a twist," I said.

CHAPTER TWENTY-TWO

After hearing about Ken Shaw's theory and including throwing in the possibility of a big shot from out-of-town trying to protect his son, Darnell said our info was starting to make sense. Now I needed to tie it in with what Darnell had discovered. "We showed our hand. Can you catch us up on where your current murder case is at and what evidence you have?"

"Why, Katie?"

"I thought you said curiosity was a positive trait?" I responded with a slight chuckle.

Darnell squinted at me and tilted his head. "I have a suspicion that it's something more than just curiosity."

"And I agree with him," Paddy said with a wink. "At least this is a case from the past, so I don't imagine you'll put yourself in any sort of danger this time."

Darnell spent the next few minutes explaining how Loretta was cleared because the call she said she received from Betty Jo jibes with what was discovered on her phone.

"Oh, so you found Betty Jo's phone?" This was news that would certainly matter to the investigation.

"Yep. That's what Jesse had yesterday when he and I stepped outside. I wanted to keep it under wraps until I could get it open. No one needed to know I had it at this point. But Neil had already given us possible passwords, and one of them worked. Saved us having to contact the cell phone company. Though we used their help in verifying that Neil was in Atlanta, as he said."

"You cleared Neil already, too?" Aubrey asked. "You verified he never left Atlanta that night?"

"That's right. His phone pinged in the area he said he had dinner with friends. They verified that. And by cell tower records, his phone was at his home until the next morning. So that cleared him."

"If you got her phone opened up, who called her that night that upset her so much that she left right after?" I asked.

"Yes, we got it opened and could see her texts and received calls. We are working on getting records for the phone number that called her around that time. As to other things we've learned, we believe the culprit may have arrived by boat, according to Jackie's photographs. From Ken and Jesse, we tried to account for boats out late that night from the lodge. Chris Pratt was night fishing Tuesday evening, so he was in a boat. I've also contacted shops that offer rentals of small craft, and they are pulling together any surveillance camera footage they might have, realizing it could have also been private boats that were used or stolen, but none reported stolen."

"So, Chris is still a suspect?" Paddy asked. "From what you've told me, it could be hard proving anything against him. It's all circumstantial."

"Darnell, I think we can kill two birds with one stone. I have a plan if you are willing to hear it. I think it could help with both cases if you're up for it."

Aubrey tapped me on the shoulder and showed me a text she sent to Loretta. I gave her a thumbs up. What an excellent idea.

"I'm all ears, Katie," Darnell said.

CHAPTER TWENTY-THREE

The Coffee Corner buzzed with energy on this sunny Saturday morning. The scent of fresh-brewed coffee wafted through the air, mixing with the inviting smell of baked goods. Our new community bulletin board, hung near the entrance, was attracting the attention of locals as they came in. Sunlight streamed in through the large front windows, casting a warm golden light over the scene.

But today, my destination wasn't the coffee shop. It was the pub restaurant to my left, where, on Saturdays and Sundays, we did a brisk brunch business.

My nerves were on edge. I couldn't deny my excitement, but at the same time, I was filled with doubt and worry. Darnell had reluctantly agreed to our plan after much convincing from Aubrey and me. Now I was starting to doubt myself. I couldn't shake the feeling that something could go wrong. Despite my reservations, I knew I needed to be present when everything unfolded.

On my way to the hostess stand, I was stopped by Nova Peters, our newest employee. She was the teenage daughter of Alan, who I had worked with on the Pirate Festival committee.

"Katie, Mr. Shaw dropped this off for you. He said it might be important. He's inside now, but wanted to be sure he didn't miss you."

"Thanks, Nova." I watched as she bent down to retrieve something from the small shelf under the hostess stand. Had Jesse brought something for me? This was a pleasant surprise.

But what she retrieved was even better. Betty Jo Turner's packet of information from Linda Pratt. A note reading *"I hope this helps. I went dumpster diving for you. Ken"* was attached to it. Just what I wanted. This might help.

I retreated to a corner in the back hall to open the clasp and look inside. Carefully redoing the clasp, I walked into the pub.

Eve, Loretta, and Peaches were seated with Neil Turner, carrying on an engaged conversation with laughter and smiles. This looked like a good time to take him the folio, explaining I'd gotten it from Chris to deliver to him, which was sort of true.

"Good morning. It's so nice you're getting to meet all of your wife's friends before you leave," I said as Neil stood to pull out a chair for me. I waved off his gesture, explaining I was going to be busy with work here this morning.

"But I do have this for you." I had removed Ken's note, and I handed the packet to Neil. "All the Secret Sisters were given a packet of letters, newspaper clippings, photographs, and memorabilia that Linda wanted them to get after her death," I said. "Chris gave Betty Jo's to me to hand off to you."

"God bless her. What a sweet gesture," Peaches said. "Linda was always our historian."

"Take a look inside," Eve encouraged Neil. "We've all enjoyed seeing the things she gave each of us."

"Thank you, Katie, for getting this to me. But I think I'll save it for later to open in the privacy of our home." He choked and softly added, "My home now."

The ladies all clasped their hands to their hearts in sympathetic gestures, murmuring their understanding.

Looking across the Saturday morning brunch crowd, I saw Ken and Jesse at a table ducked in the corner where they had a view across most of the pub.

Paddy nodded at me from the corner of the bar,

letting me know that Darnell was in place. He signaled toward Ken that it was a go.

CHAPTER TWENTY-FOUR

I began to move away from the table, saying, "Hope you have a safe trip back to Atlanta today, Neil."

"Thanks, Katie. It was a pleasure to meet you," he responded as he sat back down.

Ken and Jesse approached me. "Great brunch, as always, Katie. You guys know how to fill up a man's belly." The belly patting gesture allowed Ken to maneuver himself to look directly at Neil.

With a pinched and quizzical face, Ken said, "I think I know this handsome dude sitting with you lovely ladies. Buddy? Is that really you? Can't believe I recognized you after all these years. How's it going? I remember you from the lodge back in the day. You and your uncle were terrific fishermen. You might not remember me, but I'll bet you remember my father, Hank Shaw."

My eyes were on Neil. At first, he had smiled up at Ken. But at the use of the nickname Buddy, his expression shifted completely. His eyes hardened, and his smile tightened. He struggled to hide his reaction at being caught off guard.

"Sorry, you have the wrong guy."

"Oh, come on, you must remember. Shaw's Lodge on the Wimico River. Just a couple of miles up River Road from here. Let's see, it's gotta be forty-some years ago. That was the fall we got a bunch of new boats is how I happen to remember. Quite an unexpected purchase for my dad to make. Must have made a windfall profit that year."

"Sorry, man, I can't place that." Neil looked away from Ken and down at his half-eaten stack of pancakes. He carefully folded his napkin and laid it down next to his plate.

"Well, dang, my wife could be right. I must be getting loony in my old age. She's been telling me that for years. You were with a bunch of cousins and uncles. Took up most all our cabins. And you sure look like this guy we all called Buddy. What's your name?"

"This is Neil Turner," Peaches said. "He's from out of

town. His wife just passed away, and she was a friend of ours."

"Well, I sure got that wrong then. But you could be his twin. Sorry to bother you. Have a good day, all."

Ken and Jesse began walking toward the entrance, but then Ken spun around, reaching in his pocket for a piece of paper, and stepped back to stand beside Neil. "You look like a fisherman, though, so let me give you a special promotion in case you want to come over and check us out at Shaw's River Lodge."

Ken was good at this!

Neil began to wave his offer away, but Ken leaned in closer, literally putting the paper into Neil's hand. I was near enough to hear his whispered words. "For your own good, read this before you leave."

"Ah, sure, thanks, man, but I'm leaving town today. Like in the next fifteen minutes." Neil stood, almost tipping his chair over awkwardly, and laid his napkin on the table.

"You won't regret taking time to stop in and check us out. In fact, I bet you'll recognize the place when you stop in, and you might remember what happened there." Ken did an excellent job of adding an undercurrent of threat into those words before turning, tipping his hat, and leaving with Jesse.

And just like that, I, too, exited the restaurant and caught up with Ken and Jesse. As we drove away, I also sent a text to Darnell to let him know what was going on.

CHAPTER TWENTY-FIVE

Arriving at the fishing lodge, Ken and I walked to one of the cabins on the property. Before I went inside, he squeezed my hand, saying, "Be careful, Katie. Aubrey is already here, waiting inside the lodge with Jesse. Out of sight."

The interior of the rustic rental cabin was built for comfort and practicality after long days on the water. Much different from the purpose it served today. The cabin had a simple, open floor plan, with a few small windows that let in soft, dappled sunlight, revealing a worn plaid couch behind a coffee table holding a few well-thumbed fishing magazines.

The floorboards creaked as I entered the quiet space. The room smelled faintly of pine cleaning supplies with a hint of briny air and a smokey aroma from the cabin's old stone fireplace.

Chief Darnell sat on a chair at a small table in the functional kitchenette with pine cabinets, a mini-fridge, and a two-burner stove.

"How'd the setup go?" he asked.

"Ken was pitch perfect. He delivered the written message to Neil. I'm sure he will fall for the bait," I whispered, turning off my cell phone. "Where should we hide?"

Darnell led me to a position behind the plaid couch while he headed to what must be a small bedroom.

And none too soon because we heard Ken and Neil talking as they approached the cabin. "Yes, Mr. Turner. We can offer numerous arrangements for both large and small parties. For instance, this cabin sleeps four comfortably."

The wooden door hinges screeched as it was pushed open. Then, as soon as they'd entered, Ken's tone changed. "Thanks for letting me put on that little charade. I don't need my help to overhear us. We can talk freely in here."

"Are you sure no one is here?" Neil said. I heard his footsteps come close to the couch, and he leaned to look out the window. My heart was in my throat as I held my breath, praying he didn't look down and see me.

"No worries. It's just us here, Buddy," Ken said, "But I'm locking the door so no one interrupts us."

Footsteps sounded as someone crossed the room toward the door of the room Darnell had entered.

"You don't mind if I check it out, do you? Your note implied us discussing a private matter. I don't know if you're a man of your word."

"Go ahead. No one needs to know about this except you and me."

If Neil saw Darnell now, all would be lost. I heard a scraping sound.

Door hinges.

Shuffling.

Returning footsteps.

"What do you think you were doing back there at the pub? You had no right to interrupt my meal like that," Neil said, obviously confident they had the place to themselves.

"When I heard you were in town to take care of final arrangements for your dearly departed, and may I add murdered wife, I couldn't resist. I got word you were meeting with those broads at the pub. Perfect spot to say hello to a friend of the family. That's what I consider you, Buddy."

"I'm no friend of yours or your family."

"Oh, but your uncle, who brought you and the crew

here and your father back in Atlanta, would beg to differ. They treated us very well. Kinda like a part of the family."

A chair scraped along the floor as someone pulled it out to sit down. My guess was it was Ken. Good move. Show you're confident and in control.

"How dare you even imply anything nefarious? You don't know who you are dealing with."

"You do remember me, heh? And believe me, Buddy, I know who I'm dealing with. Now sit down, Neil. We've got a bit of talking to do."

"With my wife's proclivity to blather on when in the clutch of alcohol, I thought it could be possible she said some of the things you mentioned in your note. She had a lifelong friend in drink, and she often rambled on, forgetting where she was or who might be listening. I don't know what you heard from her, but don't believe a word of it. She'd become a hateful, spiteful person."

"That was quite a summer for you young guys, wasn't it?" Ken asked. "And to think about how it ended later that fall. What a shame. A real darn shame."

"I don't have any idea what you mean. Now why did you drag me here?"

"You couldn't keep your eyes off Tilly. Everyone saw that. She was a cute small-town gal. A little summer fling for you big-city college boys."

"Look, I wasn't a part of any relationship with that waitress. Sure she was cute, and we hung out a few times, but do you think I'm stupid enough to knock up someone like her?"

There was a long and uncomfortable pause. What was Ken doing? Was he fumbling for an answer? When I heard his next words, spoken in a calm and measured way, I knew this was planned.

"You might call your actions stupid, but I knew you were that kind of spoiled kid who would do anything to get out of a bad situation of your own making. And you almost got away with it."

"So, how'd you figure out it was me?"

CHAPTER TWENTY-SIX

"It was easy enough, even for my dearly departed father to figure out. Your nickname was Buddy. You were the *B* from Matilda Eastwood's diary. Did you even know her name, Neil, when you took her life and that of your unborn child?"

Sounds of a shove off and bang from the table hitting a cabinet, then the angry words Neil spoke, "How dare you!"

"Sit down!" Ken snapped back.

Immediately, my heart began to race, and I could feel it pounding in my throat.

Neil began pacing, his footsteps firm and measured.

"Did you follow the trial? The one where Tilly's boyfriend was charged with her murder?" Ken asked. "The police came sniffing around here. But we all kept our mouths shut per indirect orders from my father. But crafty businessman that he was, he kept pretty detailed records. Do you want to see the paper evidence I have?"

"Records of what?" Neil demanded. "What is it you're implying?"

"My father Hank was, let's say, a businessman willing to barter…silence for boats. All along he had an inkling, a suspicion of what you kids were doing, but he denied knowing any of our guests would do something like that. When he got wind of things coming out at Jimmy's trial, he knew for sure. Then, armed with incriminating information, he consulted with your father."

Neil apparently believed Ken had the paperwork because his pacing stopped, and his tone shifted to one of defeat. "Yes, I knew her name. And I knew that my father would do anything to protect me. What a stupid, arrogant kid I was."

"There you go, calling yourself stupid again." Ken chuckled. "That's the word your wife was repeating over and over to the bar crowd on Tuesday. She was pretty darn worked up."

"She suspected me of some involvement with her friend, Tilly, but I had a plausible story, and she was easy enough to manipulate. She transferred to my college and so badly wanted to believe that I'd done no wrong.

Betty Jo and I got along and, with sweet whispers in her ear of it's you I love and respect…"

My jaw clenched when I heard Ken say, "Women can be so gullible."

"You got that right," Neil said. "And Ken, man-to-man, Betty Jo was a big flirt but wouldn't put out without a commitment. She had to believe me because if she didn't, I wouldn't have married her. And that's what her end game was. So she just shut down her doubts about me, and we moved on with our lives."

"And always a little thing on the side for you, Buddy?" Ken asked. "That's still your MO, isn't it?"

I knew Ken was sticking his neck out here by relying on Loretta's old story, but it paid off. Neil's immediate response of "How did you know about…" before cutting himself off showed that the tactic worked. But would the whole confession unravel now? I quickly covered my mouth to stifle the gasp that almost escaped. We were on the verge of a breakthrough, and I couldn't risk giving away my hiding spot.

"Oh man, your wife had a whole bunch of stuff to share with anyone who would listen. She said if they find me dead, blame my husband or his latest bimbo. He's done it before, she says, and on and on," Ken said. "The sheriff had his crosshairs sighted on you, but I managed to calm things down here and misdirect him."

"So that's your angle," Neil said disdainfully. "You want more money from my family? I was home in Atlanta. I have an alibi because my cell phone was there all night. She lost her phone, and the police said it hasn't been found."

"Well, now, about that. My yard crew found it where she must have dropped it when she was stumbling around. And I'm thinking maybe I should turn it over to the police. What do you think about that? Might be pretty interesting what texts and such they find in there. My guess is you'll be brought up on charges so fast it will make your head spin. Hey, maybe on the cold case, too! No statute of limitations on murder."

"What? No way! That's completely crazy. You're lying. You would have given it to the police if you had it. Besides, your chief of police told me he thought it could have been the guy hitting on her at the bar that night. Her purse was rifled through and her money and cards stolen. So it was a robbery. They may have struggled, and she fell and hit her head before falling into the river."

"About that phone in Atlanta thing, darn if it didn't sound familiar to me. You must have watched the same murder mystery me and the missus did. The one where the guy hid his phone in a bar, so it looked like he was there during the time of the murder. Pretty clever. And you aren't so stupid. In fact, you seem pretty smart to me, sir. I mean, you drive all the way from Atlanta and then back in one night."

"How did you know that?"

"Makes sense. We saw her get a call just before she left the bar here. Now you can deny that, but if I give them her phone, I'll just bet the number can't be traced back to you. But I'll bet it will be from a throwaway phone. Probably can be traced back to where it was purchased, and there'll be store videos…"

"Stop. So this a shakedown! It's like father, like son."

"Buddy, my man. Don't go getting all worked up. I just wanted to hear what you had to say."

Darnell came out of the bedroom, saying, "And so did I."

CHAPTER TWENTY-SEVEN

As I cautiously peeked out from my hiding spot, I saw Neil Turner's expression change into one of shock and fear. His face lost its color, and his nostrils flared as he started to breathe rapidly, trying to comprehend what had just taken place.

Darnell calmly walked over to shake Ken's hand. "Thank you, sir. Good job. You saved me from having to get a confession out of Mr. Turner."

"You might have some circumstantial evidence, but you can't pin any of this on me," Neil said. "I'll plead entrapment if you try."

Darnell let out a deep, amused chuckle. "I'm not intimidated by lawyer jargon like that. Katie, are you still recording?"

I caught Darnell's eye and gave him a thumbs up as I

crawled out from behind the plaid couch and began to brush the dust bunnies from my pants. "Yes, sir. Voice recorder still on."

Neil's head spun in my direction. His voice was silenced as he took in what had just happened.

"We have enough physical evidence to convict you for your wife's murder. Your boating buddy, Jack Daniels..." Darnell slapped his thigh. "That name cracks me up every time! Think I might have a drink of Jack Daniels bourbon tonight. Anyway, his friend Scott's wife was on the river that night taking photographs and videos. Do you remember what a beautiful full moon was that night, Mr. Turner?"

"I think it's called the Wolf Moon," I added, wanting to ride Darnell's vibe.

"You could be right about that, Katie. Sure was pretty. Things show up really clear under a moon like that."

"What is she doing here?" Neil snarled.

"She's actually the person who pulled the two murders on Bonfire Beach together. I owe her a big thank you. But back to the evidence. Jackie showed me stills and video of a fishing boat tied up to the pier. And with their timestamps, they fit within the time frame of your wife's death."

"That wasn't me. I was in Atlanta. This is all bogus." Neil stood as if to leave.

But Ken pushed him back down in the chair. "Whoa there. Don't be rude to law enforcement."

Neil slapped Ken's hand off his shoulder.

"Mr. Turner, do I have to put you in handcuffs before I'm even done talking to you?"

"If you're implying what I think, I want my attorney and will say no more to you," Neil said crisply.

"I wasn't asking you anything, sir. But now, back to what I was saying. We discovered that a small boat was rented via the phone that afternoon. Nice couple of brothers run an old-style business and have a drop box for rental fees. Convenient for you, but that old-fashioned style of theirs means they didn't have a security camera either, but guess who did? The dive motel across the street installed one recently and caught the image, though a little grainy, of you leaving the harbor and then returning the boat later that night."

Neil's upper lip curled. "You couldn't have seen me. It was late at night. And it's pitch black here in the country."

"Aren't those the guys who went and got motion detector lights from Ace Hardware?" Ken asked. "You must have forgotten tripping those and getting caught in that pool of light when you picked up and dropped off the boat."

I couldn't avoid more teasing. "Buddy was probably distracted, Ken. Had a lot on his mind."

"Very true, Katie." Darnell turned back to Neil. "I'm not certain how you convinced your wife to meet you at the old pier Tuesday night. Did you give her the same sweet talk you used to lure Tilly there forty years ago?"

Neil didn't answer.

"Oh, that's right. No lawyer. No talking. Very well. Mr. Neil Turner, I'm taking you into police custody and charging you with the murders of your wife Betty Jo Turner, Matilda Eastwood, and with the murder of her unborn child."

CHAPTER TWENTY-EIGHT

It felt wonderful to get out into the fresh air.

Aubrey came running to hug me. "I'm so glad you're safe! How did it go? Did Neil confess to killing Tilly? And what about Betty Jo? Please say yes!"

"Yes. We did it, Aubrey! With help from him." I pointed to Ken as he came walking out of the cabin.

"Dad," Jesse called as he reached out to slap Ken on his back. "Did you play your part and catch Neil in the trap?"

"I think I did well enough," Ken said.

"He did an impressive job. You almost had me fooled into forgetting this was all faked. You kept up the facade and pushed the boundaries, but he fell for it."

"Hook, line, and sinker…as we in the fishing world say," Ken added.

"I'm so glad you and Darnell agreed to this charade. It couldn't have been accomplished without you and your superb ability to improvise."

"Hooray, a debt to Seaside Cove and to Tilly's family has been paid," Aubrey said. "I can't wait to hear every word of it. You got it all recorded, right? Where were you hiding?"

"Behind an old couch. And yes, got the entire thing."

We watched in silence as Darnell escorted Neil out of the cabin. Neil was in handcuffs, and his eyes squinted against the bright sunlight. When he saw us all standing there, his expression turned from resignation to defiance. He stopped and glared at us. "Is this what you all wanted?"

Darnell, sensing the tension, cleared his throat and gently pushed Neil forward. "Come on now, let's not make a scene."

As they passed by me, Darnell said, "Katie, please forward that recording to me as soon as possible. You and Aubrey have my gratitude. And you as well, Ken. Your thinking on your feet and adding some flavor to the narrative is what did the trick."

We were silent as they walked toward the side of the lodge where Darnell had hidden his cruiser.

"Come on, let's go inside. Chris Pratt has been wanting to check out and head back home," Ken said.

Then he called out, "Hey, Chief, is Chris authorized to leave town now?"

"He's free to go," Darnell said. "Can I give you a ride back to town, Katie?"

Neil stood with his head hanging down, averting his eyes from everyone.

"With that man in the back seat? No, thank you. I'll ride back with Aubrey."

"But first a coffee with us?" Jesse asked. "I think my dad needs to decompress."

"Sure," Aubrey said. "But we've got some big-time celebrating to do. And lots of people to share this news with."

She was right about people who would be happy to hear this news. Jimmy Conrad was on top of my list. What he had been through was hard to imagine. But with Bernice's help, he seemed to have managed to live a good life. I tried to think what Frances Eastwood's reaction would look like. Something very different from Jimmy's. She'd probably do a foot-stomping happy dance while shouting yoo-hoo. In all the years, she never retreated, like Tuesday at the football field where she called out the Secret Sisters. I hoped none of them would carry guilt about what could have been done differently. Like Linda's note to Eve, this resolution should help bring closure.

The river, a deep blue-gray, reflected the clouds moving in with the sun breaking through intermittently, casting a golden glow over the grounds of the lodge. The pale mist that hung over the river earlier was gone. A hawk glided above us, and in the distance, a heron called. A cool January breeze made me pull my jacket closer and hook my elbow with Aubrey's as we walked back up the lodge.

"Mission accomplished," Aubrey said. "Hard to believe what all has happened in less than a week. The Secret Sisters should be told that the murders of two of their group have been solved."

"Agreed. But first, a cup of coffee with Ken and Jesse."

CHAPTER TWENTY-NINE

A warm, welcoming scent of coffee wafted through the air, drawing us to the dining room where Ken had set a table for the four of us to gather away from the early Saturday night diners who occupied tables near the huge windows looking out toward the river. Ken greeted some of the dinner guests with a warm smile, quickly transitioning back to his professional demeanor as though he had not just helped drag a confession out of a murderer.

When Ken noticed Aubrey and I had taken seats by Jesse at the table, he quickly joined us, thanking me for allowing him to be a part of this moment. Apparently, what happened all those years ago troubled him on and off over the years, but he could never find a way to make it right. The Turner family members never returned to the camp, and Hank said just let it be, assuring him that there was really no proof that Buddy did it, but his father wanted to make sure even the possibility never rose up.

"I didn't know all of it early on. I was young and more interested in fishing and getting Marge to marry me. Then, when the trial came and went, and Jimmy was free, I didn't dig deeper."

"Dad, what did Darnell mean by you added flavor?"

"Ah, let's just say I used the things that came to me at the moment. Maybe shaded them a little to make Katie's idea work," Ken said.

"Is Chris still here?" Aubrey asked.

"Nope. He hit the road as fast as he could. I really can't blame him. What a hornet's nest his mother's last wishes had stirred up," Jesse said.

"But now the crimes are solved," I said. "Someone should let Tilly's sister know."

Ken volunteered to call Frankie with the good news since he knew her better than Aubrey and I. He also wanted to take the opportunity to explain his father's role in the original deception and apologize for it. This would be a difficult conversation but also cathartic for him. He left to make the call from the lodge's office for privacy.

Aubrey suggested we get the remaining Secret

Sisters together tonight and fill them in on everything that happened today after Neil left the pub. "And maybe Vincent would like to join us," she said. "I'll set it up for them to come to the house. Oh, and I'm going to step outside right now and call Jimmy and Bernice. It's hard to believe how this has all happened in just a few days. We solved a cold case murder!"

Through the large dining room windows, Jesse and I watched Aubrey settle into one of the Adirondack chairs and take a sip of her coffee before opening her cell phone to begin making calls.

"So, it's just you and me, kid," Jesse said. "You must have been pretty creative with that note you had Dad deliver to Neil."

"It had to do the trick," I said. "If Neil didn't stop here to talk with Ken, he'd have gone back to Atlanta, and it would have been very difficult to get him to confess to anything."

"That was a very clever scheme you set up to get Neil to talk. You took some risks to get the truth out, and I admire that," Jesse said with a playful glint in his dark eyes.

"We both took risks. Wait until you hear your father on the recording I captured. Like when he asked if Neil wanted to see the incriminating paperwork he had. I don't know if it would have stood up to the law."

Jesse's lips curled upwards as he released a low, amused chuckle. "Dad showed me the accounting books and asked me my opinion about their value as evidence. Most of that could have been explained away by a good lawyer. Grandpa and Neil's family were especially cautious about keeping their exchange of items of value away from prying eyes."

"Want to hear some of the recording I made?" I'd forwarded the recording to Darnell already and now I sent a copy to Jesse. He put his earbuds in and began to listen.

I couldn't resist stealing glances at his face as he reacted to what he was hearing. His range of expressions as he listened was mesmerizing, from the raised arch of his eyebrows in surprise to the crooked grin that played on his lips and his eyes widening in shock. He laughed, absently brushing a lock of his silky hair away from his forehead, and stopped the recording to say, "I'm hearing those flavorful words! I've got to say this is a side of Dad that I've never seen." Then he hit the play button again.

There was no denying his good looks, and I had to consciously look away before he caught me staring.

I found it hard to believe that this was all that had happened from that first day when Ella said we had to stop and see what was going on. That reminded me I should let Ella know how this worked out.

Jesse finished listening before I said, "Now don't get a big head over what I'm about to tell you, but that day when Ella and I were driving, and we heard the sirens on River Road, my first concern was it could be you who needed the ambulance."

Jesse turned his head toward me, his warm brown eyes pulling me in. "That's really sweet of you," he said with a smile.

I cleared my throat anxiously, attempting to settle the fluttering feeling in my stomach caused by his intense gaze. "Ella let me know it didn't involve you. You know she has that intuitive, almost psychic way about her, don't you?"

"I do," he said. "She's different, like she can read thoughts."

His words made me feel as though he could decipher my own thoughts in that moment, although I wasn't sure what they were telling him. I quickly refocused on the story at hand. "But then she also warned me. She said I must stop because something bad is happening to someone I know. And so that's where this all started."

Jesse touched me under the chin, lifting my head up to meet his gaze. "I'm glad she was with you. What you've done for not only Jimmy and Frankie but for our community shows me your heart. And don't go saying you did it for the fun of solving a cold case. It's so much more than that."

The sudden ring of my phone broke the silence and caused us both to jump. I glanced at it and didn't pick up, but the mood had shifted.

Ken returned to tell me that Frankie didn't have the words to express how thankful she was. Aubrey came back inside to say she'd gotten hold of everyone and asked if I was ready to leave.

Jesse wrapped me in a hug and urged me to head out. He reminded me that people were waiting for me, even though all I wanted was to stay here with him and watch the Wolf Moon rise.

CHAPTER THIRTY

Before heading back to Seaside Cove, I suggested we make a quick stop at Ella's. I wanted to fill her in on what had happened. Aubrey was eager to see the place, as she had never been there. While she wandered the grounds, playing with the goats and feeding the horses carrots, I shared details with Ella of how things unfolded.

"And you were even mentioned in Tilly's diary," I said.

"Ah yes, the beginnings of my travel into the world of tarot card reading. To be honest, I don't remember specifics about her reading. As a reader, I facilitate self-discovery. We helped the querent find clarity in the areas she had concerns with or questions about. She was just a young woman, and she was seeking guidance in the relationship realm. But she had difficulty expressing herself, opening up. Tarot is not fortune telling, and I'm afraid that was what she came to me for."

"I guess relationships are super important to girls at that age," I said. "Well, we'd better be going. Aubrey and I are going to explain all the intrigue and mystery of how we got to the point of Neil Turner being arrested for both murders."

Aubrey dropped me back at Paddy's Pub to pick up my cart while she went ahead home to put together some appetizers for our meetup with the Secret Sisters later. Paddy was inside and happy to hear things had gone well. I mentioned that Darnell might join him for a bourbon tonight to celebrate a job well done.

Next, I swung by Maeve's cottage to inform her that the cold case and recent murder had been solved. As I pulled up, Winnie rushed over to greet me. She seemed particularly intent on getting out what she wanted to say.

"Remember, I told you I'd ponder on why Loretta was actin' so darn peculiar? Well, something dawned on me. I was volunteering at the hospital coffee spot Wednesday and who do I see strollin' through the lobby but Loretta? Now mind you, this is a small town, and lots of them needing doctor tests get sent here. I ask her what she thinks 'bout that whole mess down at Bonfire Beach, and she tells me she's got bigger fish to fry. And I'm thinkin', what could be bigger than a dang murder? Then it hits me—I saw her at the hospital last month too! Now I reckon she's goin' through some doctoring herself, and that's what's got her all out of sorts."

"That makes sense," Maeve said. "Remember, she left the book club because she didn't feel well."

"Aubrey and I are getting together tonight with Eve, Peaches, and Loretta. Do you think I should ask her about her health?" I asked.

"That's a tough one," Maeve said. "Some people are very guarded about health issues. She knows she has friends she can talk to when she's ready."

Winnie shook her head. "And some folks want to be asked, don't they? Those kinds don't bring it up on their own. I say pull her aside, look her in the eye, and ask."

* * *

Aubrey had carefully arranged the newspapers detailing Tilly's murder, her diary, and copies of photos and register pages from our outing at Shaw's Lodge on the dining room table. In the center of it all was a spread of appetizers.

Rather surprisingly, Raven was attracted to Vincent. As soon as he sat down, she climbed on her back legs and began kneading his legs, showing she wanted to be picked up and cuddled.

"I hope she's not bothering you," I said.

"Not at all," Vincent replied with a small smile, gently scooping Raven up into his lap. "My dearly departed wife always had at least two cats in our home. I think I may consider getting one."

"The Humane Society will be holding an adopt a pet event later this spring," I offered. "Might be a good chance for you to see what they have."

Vincent nodded thoughtfully as he absently stroked Raven and took in the women who were here to learn about our findings.

The ladies were in awe of what we had done and thankful that we helped fulfill Linda's written desire that her friend and roommate's murder be solved. They were fascinated to read Tilly's diary, remembering many of the things she'd written about. They were moved by her last entries, knowing that within hours, she would no longer be filling in the lined pages with her hopes and dreams.

The photographs of guests of Shaw's from years ago

caught their eye as well. They pointed out local guides they knew and were amazed at how renowned the place had been.

Everyone wanted to hear the recording of the scene in the cabin today after hearing how I hid behind the couch to record it. This was the first time I'd listened to it myself. And again, I was so impressed with how Ken handled the entire thing. No wonder Neil believed him.

"I'll have to tell Marge she's got an actor on her hands," Peaches said. "I was beginning to think this was real myself! Ken really pulled out all the plugs to make Neil believe him. Was all of that true?"

"I'm not sure. But it might take a white lie to trip up a liar like Neil," I said.

"You signaled us not to push on about Betty Jo's packet this morning at Paddy's," Eve said. "Did you see what was inside?"

"I did peek. It was similar to yours except to be much more pointed about Linda's intuition that Betty Jo knew much more than she ever revealed or admitted to. And certainly, never spoke of. It wouldn't have mattered at the point we were at because the setup at the cabin was already in play and had to happen before Neil left town."

Vincent said, "The fact you two narrowed it down to Neil was impressive. How did that come about?"

"Loretta, do you want to repeat what you told me yesterday?" I asked.

"No, why don't you go ahead," Loretta said.

She seemed better today. Maybe Winnie was mistaken about her being ill. It might have truly been the stress. Especially knowing what she'd kept to herself all these years. Peaches and Vincent hadn't heard the story, so I briefly explained what Loretta witnessed many years ago in Atlanta.

Then Aubrey took over to say how last night she'd texted Loretta three things—a photo of Neil, AKA Buddy, when he was at the fishing lodge, then one from his college yearbook, and last, a recent LinkedIn photograph of him. "And that's where Loretta's identification of Neil at the time she ran into him and Betty Jo in Atlanta helped. Loretta saw him in the in-between times, and her verification that it was the same person tied all the faces together into one nasty murderer."

"Do you think Betty Jo knew it was him all along?" Vincent asked.

"That's a tough one to answer," I said. "He provided her with plausible deniability with the stories he gave her."

"You're so right," Eve said. "I remember well how, despite all her flirting and trying to take away local boys from their girlfriends, none of them were her final aspiration. And making that move to Emory midterm sealed it with Neil. Plus, they really never came back here together, so no one was the wiser about how or where they met."

"And I can't recall her ever saying just where they did meet. Except Neil said they met at college."

"Eve, a question about that book *Where the Road Ends*. Your letter from Linda said you used stories from Seaside Cove to write it. Did you?" Loretta asked. "Was the Sharon character really based on me?"

"That's a tale for another time, my friends." Eve's voice trailed off as she glanced around the room with a sly smile. "An author never reveals all of her secrets. Besides, I believe our brains have been sufficiently exercised for the week, and tomorrow is another day."

CHAPTER THIRTY-ONE

Hannah did a fantastic job covering the resolution of the Tilly Eastwood cold case for the Cove Gazette. She interviewed locals who remembered the tragic death of the girl, piecing together a narrative of a town on edge, filled with rumors and suspicions. Her reporting added depth and context to the time period in which it had taken place. The fact that the man who would be going on trial in that case was also being charged with first-degree murder in the recent death of his wife added an unexpected twist to the story.

Throw in the fact that the two events happened in the same location, and it was bound to attract the attention of the national news media. This is likely how it caught the eye of a producer from a popular syndicated television show that focused on unsolved crime mysteries from around the country.

With a television show production company coming to town, things were stirred up the next few weeks. The crew stayed at the Fulton Inn and some of them even extended their stay to enjoy all the things, besides murder, that Seaside Cove had to offer. From relaxing at the beach on Horseshoe Island to fishing on the Wimico. From renting bikes for riding on the River Road to indulging in the fresh seafood offerings at Gator's Grill.

We had a watch party upstairs in the Waterford Room when the episode was broadcast and invited anyone who wanted to watch with us to the Waterford Room that evening. The place was packed!

"I'm glad we decided to do this," Maeve said. "It's a way to honor what you and Aubrey achieved."

"Thanks, Auntie, but we had tons of help. Vincent, the Secret Sisters, Darnell, and Ken. I'm so happy they were interviewed for the show."

"But who will land on the cutting floor?" Aubrey said, raising a cautionary finger in the air. "It better not be me because I can't tell you the effort it took to put on false eyelashes for my day under the lights. I searched television camera makeup tips and I couldn't believe how much work goes into that. I have new respect for makeup artists."

"And you got a new outfit for tonight," I said. "You look great! Maybe someone will want your autograph."

"Stop!" Aubrey said, with a tilt of her head and a coy glance over her shoulder. "Do you think they might? But seriously, my friend, this is pretty darn cool! It'll put Seaside Cove on the map."

"It has already," Darnell said as he joined us. "I've been getting more reports of vandalism at Bonfire Beach. The owners of the property live out of town and are not very hands-on. Maybe they'll decide to completely wipe out the pier and the old fishing shack after all this."

"I hope not," I said. Then I wondered why that was my first reaction. Couldn't it be a place for the town to take over and make into a small park? Or would the murders there forever haunt the site?

Paddy welcomed our guests and made sure everyone had a good view with three televisions screens brought in.

Liam dimmed the lights, and the introductory music to the show came on. A collective moment of recognition rolled through the audience as a drone shot of Seaside Cove appeared on the screens, and the narrator began his story.

"Deep in the Florida Panhandle lies the small town of…" We were silent, mesmerized by the camera shots and angles, the background music, and the story being told.

The victim was introduced by Tilly's sister, Frankie. I knew it took a lot of convincing, primarily by Ken Shaw, to get her to agree to speak to the filmmaker. Ken convinced her that she was integral to the story and should be proud of what was accomplished. Her interview was taken at dusk at Bonfire Beach with a fire burning in the stone fire pit. The flames created an eerie feeling, darkening the background behind her. She was filmed holding a photograph of her sister, and all of us watching felt the emotion she was experiencing. The room was quiet and there may have been a few tears shed. But Frankie remained stoic throughout, her face emotionless as she watched herself on screen. We were glad she came tonight, so she didn't watch this alone.

Next, we were taken to the high school football field with overlays of yearbook photos and actual grainy video that someone in town provided to the production company of Jimmy Conrad playing quarterback in a game with a quick glimpse of Tilly, Peaches, and Betty Jo in the cheerleading squad. Of course, Jimmy was interviewed for the show and parts of his interview were added over the video of him playing football. It was eerie and poignant to imagine what he went through. Especially when he spoke of the painful period he experienced being tried for the murder of his girlfriend. Bernice held his hand through the entire episode.

The cameras were rolling as Aubrey and I shared our stories and memories. The producer of the show had sat down with us at Aubrey's dining room table with the old newspapers that sparked our journey spread in front of us. Vincent also joined us, bringing his unique perspective and adding depth to our discussion.

The remaining Secret Sisters were interviewed, as was Chief Darnell, and of course, the crew filmed at Shaw's River Lodge. For the climactic reenactment scene inside the small cabin, an actor played Neil Turner, but all the crew agreed that Ken should play himself and he stole the show! Marge looked on with pride as we all saw and heard the tense climatic scene scripted from the recording made that day. And then the show ended, the lights came up and there was a loud round of applause.

The Seaside Cove community was deeply touched by the moment. A sense of relief seemed to wash over everyone before they started to disperse, many stopping to talk with Jimmy, Vincent, Frankie, and Ken, the individuals most connected to Tilly's case.

Now that this viewing was done, I could look

forward to Valentine's Day preparation, especially here in the Waterford room. It would be transformed into a romantic space for couples to celebrate. White tablecloths, a beautiful floral arrangement, and flickering candles would adorn every table. Slim and Maeve had worked up a special menu just for the occasion, featuring some extra scrumptious desserts. Mel the mannequin was ready to greet guests, dressed as the cutest cupid. All of our tables were booked!

When Grace Norris suggested we do a joint promotion for Valentine's Day, I was all in. Grace had officially opened her Grace Guest House. Just last year, she had seized the opportunity to fulfill her lifelong dream of running a guest house when, in a surprise twist of fate, an empty mansion, once the grand home of the wealthy McCracken banking family, was inherited by Ruby Flowers. They worked out a financial arrangement, and Grace was off and running, lovingly remodeling the stately mansion, keeping its historic charm while updating it with a warm, welcoming decor. Grace's attention to detail was obvious throughout the high-ceilinged rooms filled with antique furniture. Soft, pastel hues were used in paint colors and furnishings, like the handmade quilts on the guest beds and the wicker furniture on the large veranda, to reflect the coastal location.

Aubrey had finally convinced me to make a New Year resolution. Any resolution would do, she'd playfully taunted. When I explained that I wanted it to be a practical and achievable one because I failed so often at others, she said her suggestion was simple. You just have to do one thing. Buy a new golf cart this year!

And I did it! I hoped my new customized golf cart was ready before my two best friends from Ireland arrived for a visit with me in Florida. They were finally coming to America, and I could hardly contain my excitement at the thought of seeing them again. There was so much catching up for us to do.

Once the pink and red decorations of Valentine's Day were put away, our beloved Mel the Mannequin shed his cupid costume and was dressed in a festive green leprechaun outfit. A pot of gold was placed at his feet, ready for the upcoming St. Patrick's Day festivities both at the pub and throughout the town.

The countdown to St. Patrick's Day had begun!

ABOUT THE AUTHOR

Here are a few ways to reach me…I'd love to stay in connected!

Please <u>sign up for my monthly newsletter</u>. I'll share things about my life…both personal as Brenda Felber and professionally as my pen name Suzanne Bolden.
Like/follow Suzanne on her Facebook page

If you follow me on these two, you'll be automatically notified when new releases are available.
Bookbub
<u>Amazon Author Central</u>

Check out my website <u>www.suzannebolden.com</u>

Thank you for reading my books. If you enjoyed them, a review is much appreciated!

ALSO BY SUZANNE BOLDEN

Katie Murphy Cozy Mystery Series

#1 Pour Decisions

#2 Pick Yar Poison

#3 Raising Spirits

#4 Auld Lang Stein

#5 A Wee Lepre-Con

#6 Paws for a Pint

7 The Elf Did It

#8 Matrimony and Malice

#9 Read Between the Lines